A TIME TO KILL

As the terrorist Muli recovered, lunged, and thrust with his knife, David Holden vaulted to one side, his leg sweeping out and knocking Muli off his feet.

As Muli started to rise, David was on him, his own knife flashing in the firelight. Screams came from Muli—like the screams of the dying women—and something flew away from his body. His knife—but something else. "Ohh—" Lang choked on his breath. They were Muli's fingers.

Lang heard David shout as his knife hand rose, then hammered downward.

Charlie Lang, FLNA mastermind, screamed again—because of where David stabbed Muli: The knife was buried in Muli's face.

ENTRAPMENT

Jerry Ahern

A DELL BOOK

Published by
Dell Publishing
a division of
Bantam Doubleday Dell
Publishing Group, Inc.
666 Fifth Avenue
New York, New York 10103

ISBN: 0-440-20329-5

Printed in the United States of America

Published simultaneously in Canada

May 1989

10 9 8 7 6 5 4 3 2 1
OPM

*To Rick, Keith, Herb, Grady, "Wild Bill," and all
the folks at WJJC,
all the best . . .*

CHAPTER

1

A wind blew stiff and chill from the north, drying the sweat over his body almost instantly; but that did not make him shiver. The assault of the white foam-edged surf advanced relentlessly inland against the sand, the moon low on the horizon and so full and bright that malformed shadows were strewn along the beach by those, like David Holden, who walked its length. As he sidestepped the water to keep his boots dry, the packing for the recently rebandaged gunshot wound to his right calf slipped a little. That made him shiver. He kept walking, however, with Luther Steel beside him. Steel reminded Holden in hushed tones, "If anyone comes up to us, let me do the talking."

Holden said nothing, his teeth gritted against the pain.

Black and dark-green camouflage-painted helicopter gunships were ranked northward along the beach. David Holden counted eight in all as he limped toward the nearest of them. He flexed the fingers of his right hand inside his black leather glove. The grazing wound across the fleshy inside of his right upper arm caused him almost no pain and required only a modest bandage; but he subcon-

sciously favored the arm a little because of the wound
and some resultant stiffness.

"How are you feeling?" Steel hissed.

"Okay," Holden answered. He wasn't actually lying to
the black FBI agent, Holden told himself. The stiffness in
his fingers was merely an annoyance and was going away;
the grazing wound across his left rib cage was deep and
raw but bothered him only if he moved wrong or if his
shoulder holster shifted and the butt of the Beretta Compact hit him there. The leg wound hurt; each step he took
sent a tremor of pain upward, precipitating more of the
cold sweat that dried almost instantly in the wind. And
then the process would repeat. Maybe Rosie had been
right; he should have left well enough alone and not attempted this. But his answer to Steel's question, relatively
speaking, was an honest one, all things considered.

Two Patriots had been killed, five others were seriously
wounded, three police officers had been killed, five
wounded, and FBI agent Bill Runningdeer was in serious
but stable condition from the wounds to his left arm and
shoulder. Even Rosie Shepherd had taken some lumps, a
deep grazing wound across the top of her left shoulder
("Best excuse I ever had not to wear a bra for a coupla
days.") and some painful but not terribly serious sprains
and bruises to her left ankle and foot when one of the
FLNA-ers' bikes went out of control as someone shot the
man out of the saddle. Rosie could have been hurt more
seriously, and David Holden was grateful she was
not. . . .

*A gray Lincoln, stretched to limousine proportions,
turned the corner. It was Harris Gamby's car.*

*The car parked, no one left the vehicle for several sec-
onds, then the door on the front passenger side opened and*

a security man stepped out. He walked toward where David Holden, Rosie Shepherd, Luther Steel, Bill Runningdeer, and Clark Pietrowski stood.

"Are you David Holden, sir?"

"Yes."

"Mr. Gamby would like a moment of your time, sir."

David Holden shrugged the H&K submachine gun behind his back on its sling, then followed the security man toward the gray, stretched Lincoln.

The rear door opened and Holden cautiously leaned inside, his right arm still a little stiff from the gunshot wound. "Professor Holden?"

Harris Gamby looked smaller than he did in his photographs.

"Yes, Mr. Gamby."

"Odd, about being an American, isn't it? I hate everything you stand for, and you likely hate everything I stand for. But here we are, both of us interested in this election being held and the voters deciding. For that, I commend you, sir. I suppose, should I win, I should thank you for it. But I imagine we'd both consider that hypocritical, wouldn't we?"

Gamby smiled.

Holden smiled too. "Yes, I suppose we would, sir."

Gamby extended his hand. Holden took it.

David Holden turned and walked away, hearing the door slam, looking back as Harris Gamby exited his vehicle. His security people, the uniformed police, and a group of Patriots who Rosie signaled into motion fell in around him.

Still cameras flashed. Video cameras hummed. Reporters tried bursting through the ranks of police, Patriots, and security to reach Gamby, firing questions toward him, an occasional "No comment" from Gamby heard over the babble of questions.

The mother superior of the school's adjoining convent waited at the door of the polling place, Gamby shook her hand, then walked inside.

Luther Steel whispered, "I'm glad that's half over."

David Holden looked at his Rolex when he heard the first rumble of a motorcycle. It was eight minutes after six. Already a dozen or more voters had lined up, were filtering inside.

The first bike came around the corner, then more streaming after it, a van and then another one, and another one coming.

Clark Pietrowski shouted over the increasing roar as he drew his revolver, "Betcha even money they're not here to vote!"

"Not in the usual way." David Holden nodded.

Luther Steel broke into a run toward the school, shouting to the uniformed police, "Get inside, guard Gamby and the rest of the voters! Move it!"

Bill Runningdeer shifted back his raincoat, the Uzi appearing.

Rosie Shepherd swung her M-16 forward.

The sun winked up over the artificial horizon created by the steeple of the church that abutted the school building.

It would be a hot day, Holden thought absently as he started walking down the street, moving his H&K submachine gun forward into an assault position, working the tumbler off safe to full auto.

The lead bike stopped.

The other bikes immediately behind it stopped.

The vans formed a wedge blocking the street. Ralph Kaminsky was shouting something unintelligible through his bullhorn. Luther Steel ran up.

Rosie Shepherd and David Holden stood shoulder to shoulder.

A slimy voice called out from one of the vans over a P.A. system. "There's not gonna be a damned election!"

David Holden looked at Rosie. She smiled.

Clark Pietrowski laughed, "Go ahead, Holden."

Luther Steel murmured, "Right on!"

David Holden took a step forward, Rosie beside him, the others flanking him. Holden glanced back once as the street behind him swelled with Patriots, some of the uniformed cops, and even Kaminsky's SWAT people.

David Holden called back, "Maybe not today, maybe not tomorrow, or even the next day—but you and your people—FLNA, whatever you call yourselves—you lose."

The lead biker squirmed in his saddle.

Somebody near Holden coughed.

The sun moved rapidly upward over the church and school and the residential homes surrounding them.

The FLNA spokesman inside one of the vans shouted over his P.A. system, "Get 'em!"

Somebody fired the first shot.

David Holden sidestepped left to block Rosie with his body as he opened fire and peeled three of the motorcycle riders into the street. Rosie fired from behind him, the M-16 roaring so close to his left ear that his head rang with the sound. Clark Pietrowski held his revolver one-handed and straight out in front of him, firing, catching one of the lead bikers and hurtling him from the saddle.

Holden emptied the H&K submachine gun, bringing down two more bikers, blowing out the front tire on a third man's machine, the motorcycle crashing into one of the vans. Holden reached his M-16 forward and flipped the selector to auto, bringing it to his shoulder, firing short bursts into the windshield of the nearest van, shattering the *windshield. The van swerved wildly out of the street, bouncing the curb and crashing into the front of a house. As one of the van's occupants stepped out, a submachine gun in his hands, a woman suddenly appeared on the front porch of the house and shot him in the face with a shotgun.*

Holden emptied the M-16 into the second van, letting it fall empty to his side, drawing the Desert Eagle. He thumbed back the hammer and fired, ripping one of the bikers from his machine. Holden stepped aside as the riderless motorcycle crashed past him.

His right leg took a hit and Holden stumbled forward. Rosie dropped to her knees beside him, still firing. "I'm all right!" Holden shouted, his right calf feeling as though it were on fire. Holden stabbed the Desert Eagle forward, fired, killing another one of the men from the sidetracked van. Holden got to his feet. He fired again, killing another biker.

Holden emptied the Desert Eagle into the second van, the van swerving away, impacting a fire plug as it bounced over the curb, overturned, and exploded. Holden put his left arm around Rosie's shoulders, drawing her close to him as the wash of heat from the explosion passed over them.

The Desert Eagle empty, Holden holstered it, drew both Beretta pistols. Rosie's .45 boomed beside him. Luther Steel wrestled a man from his motorcycle, kicked him twice in the face, grabbed up an Uzi, and swung into the saddle as he wrestled the machine upright. Steel charged the machine into the thickest of the motorcycle-riding FLNA-ers.

Bill Runningdeer and Clark Pietrowski stood back to back, Runningdeer firing his Uzi, Pietrowski closing the cylinder of his revolver, firing point-blank into an

FLNA-er charging toward him, bringing the FLNA-er down.

FLNA-ers were coming at them from all sides. Holden, a pistol in each hand, fired, fired again and again and again. Rosie stumbled, lurched against him. "I'm all right!" But there was blood on the left side of her neck.

Holden's pistols were empty.

An FLNA-er jumped from his motorcycle, Holden side-stepped him and crashed the butt of the larger Beretta down across the man's skull.

Holden rammed one of the twenty-round magazines into the larger Beretta, no time to reload the smaller one. His left fist wrenched the Defender knife free.

A knot of FLNA-ers closed around them.

"I love you!" Rosie Shepherd shouted to him.

He knew that. David Holden took the right side, Rosie the left, Holden firing his pistol as he waded forward, and as he closed with them, using the knife.

He felt a searing pain across his left rib cage just below his shoulder holster, then a wash of cold over him. He stumbled but didn't fall.

He saw Rosie, her M-16 turned around, swatting with it as her attackers closed with her.

Holden's pistol was empty.

He threw himself onto the men surrounding Rosie, hammering at their skulls with the butt of his pistol, ramming the knife into every opening of flesh.

A rifle butt glanced off the side of his head where he had the small head wound from before. He sagged to his knees. As the man closed for the kill Holden straight-armed him in the crotch with his knife, letting the man fall past him.

Holden pushed a fresh magazine into the submachine gun, dropping the empty one into the street.

To his feet, firing three- and four-round bursts.

The FLNA-ers were falling back.

Rosie Shepherd limped toward him, using her rifle like a cane, her submachine gun and her .45 in her right fist.

Runningdeer mounted a motorcycle and joined Steel, the left sleeve of Runningdeer's raincoat stained red with blood.

David Holden hurt all over. As he extended his left arm, folded it across Rosie's shoulders, the grazing wound along his left rib cage sent tremors through him. He closed his eyes against the light-headedness for an instant.

As he opened his eyes he looked toward the school. On the flagpole—he didn't know who had put it there—was the same emblem as the one emblazoned on the sleeve of his BDU jacket. The flag.

The election for mayor of Metro was won only because there was a free election. It was lost for Holden because Harris Gamby, a man who stood for everything David Holden believed had gone wrong in the United States, won. Yet Gamby had won only after Roger Costigan had been exposed. That exposure wouldn't have been possible without the Patriots. Gamby was the choice of an outraged people with no other choice remaining, a people outraged when they learned that Costigan, the candidate they had supported, the candidate who outwardly embraced the goals that made America great and could help to save the nation now, was a fraud, a pawn of the Front for the Liberation of North America, ready to hand government and public trust into the hands of the enemy.

And it was finally, decisively lost when the politically naive and dangerous Harris Gamby, his only virtue his honesty, was assassinated the day following his election when a suicide pilot crashed an explosives-laden aircraft into Gamby's home. What had the FLNA promised the pilot? Or threatened him with?

More than an election was lost.

And now a task force of Justice Department Special Operations Groups was assembling on the beach eight miles south of the docks that served Cedar Ridge Islands, the exclusive resort that had been turned into an FLNA front. It was the first stop on the North American infiltration route used by foreign nationals coming to lead FLNA units around the United States, Canada, and Mexico.

A helicopter would leave the posh resort around midnight, fly out to sea and rendezvous with either a submarine or a trawler, then fly the human cargo back to Cedar Ridge Islands. There, forged documents of the highest quality manufactured under the supervision of master forger Charlie Lang, who ran Cedar Ridge Islands for the unwitting owners, were delivered to the foreign nationals. Everything from clothing to deodorant was provided to aid in their assimilation and easy movement to their posts. Once on site, they established contact with FLNA leaders already in place and the urban gangbangers and criminals who were their well-financed military units. Each man's background included terrorism, subversion, and sabotage. They were the cream of an international network dedicated to the destruction of the United States.

Holden stood beside the nearest chopper, the collar of his black M-65 field jacket turned up, not against the wind but to hide his face. He was, despite a bizarre alliance with the President of the United States through FBI Director Rudolph Cerillia and Special Agent-in-Charge for the Metro Task Force Luther Steel, the most wanted man in America.

When the FLNA onslaught began, Holden's family was among the first casualties. His wife, Elizabeth, his daughters Meg and little Irene, his son, Dave, were all murdered when the commencement exercises at Thomas Jefferson University were hit. Dr. David Holden's life as a professor of history who supplemented his meager income through illustrations for science fiction stories and the occasional cover assignment was just as lost as the lives of his loved ones.

For some odd reason as he stood there on the beach trying to look inconspicuous while Luther Steel conversed with one of the unit commanders, David Holden thought of Rufus Burroughs. Burroughs, a black Metro cop and Vietnam veteran, lost his wife that same day in that same attack; she was to have been awarded her master's degree.

Burroughs had been one of the prime movers in the formation of the Patriots. At first nothing more than a group of concerned citizens interested in aiding law enforcement and the military in combating the FLNA, when conventional law enforcement and unwieldy military operations failed miserably, the Patriots began using arms stored for self-protection to strike back. Because the Patriots were effective where the organized forces of government were not, they were vilified in the liberal media, condemned in the halls of Congress, outlawed because of their direct action—albeit their direct action worked.

Rufus Burroughs died during the successful foiling of an FLNA plot to precipitate a nuclear meltdown at Plant Wright. Such a disaster could have contaminated the entire Metro area and caused untold deaths. David Holden, new to the Patriots—forced to join after he was arrested for unlawful use of a weapon and other unspecified charges because he fought back during an FLNA terror attack—became the Patriot leader. Rose Shepherd, like Rufus Burroughs a police officer forced out, branded a criminal because she was a Patriot, was Rufus Burroughs's second-in-command, became Holden's. But she became Holden's in other ways—his mistress and lover, his only rest and happiness in a fight some Americans had no will to win and others died to win.

As some of the despair and pain conceived in the murder of his family softened in the few moments he could almost forget when he lay in Rosie's arms, while battling the FLNA the skills he had learned as a navy SEAL team leader gradually returned. His SEALs background and his three years on Metro PD while in graduate school after leaving active duty were not nearly enough to combat the FLNA.

But he tried.

That was all any American could do, he told himself. He tried and would keep trying until the FLNA was a bitter memory, enemies of freedom dead or vanquished—or until he died, still trying. And his death seemed most likely. That was what added special urgency to his deepening love for Rosie Shepherd. Death for them was more than inevitable; it was almost palpable.

"Is he over there?"

"That's right. The third gunship from the end. See?"

"Yeah, I see him. Thanks," Luther Steel said, concluding the conversation that, on one level of consciousness, David Holden thought had worn on forever.

Hunching more deeply into the collar of his coat, Holden fell in beside Steel. The pain in Holden's right leg returned with a vengeance. "He said my friend Biff Loman is up here."

"Biff Loman?"

"The man I was telling you about, in charge of the

D.C. area SWAT team for the Bureau. He's very compe-
tent, and a man we can trust. He's the only one out here I
would trust because he's the only one I know well
enough. One of these others might turn you in. Leg killing you?"

"Yeah."

"You should have listened to Detective Shepherd."

"I'm beginning to think that myself."

"Any problems, flash Bill Runningdeer's I.D., as I told
you; and pray a lot."

Holden felt a smile touch the corners of his mouth as
he looked at Luther Steel. Steel started to laugh as he
called out: "Yo! Biff! Biff Loman! Hey!"

A man whose physique fit the general description of a
single-door refrigerator turned away from the group of
four heavily armed men in SWAT black BDUs with
whom he had evidently been conversing and seemed to
stare at Steel and Holden for a moment. He caught up an
M-16 from inside the open fuselage door of the gunship
next to him and started toward them. Holden stopped
walking when Steel did. Holden's leg began throbbing
like a toothache.

The large man—Biff Loman—said in an impossibly
gravely voice, "You're David Holden, the renegade college professor. I admire your work, sir. But you're under
arrest."

"Don't do that, Biff," Luther Steel said, putting a hand
against Loman's chest.

"And why not?"

"Trust me on it," Steel said. Lowering his voice, he
added, "Or I'll shoot your ass."

Biff Loman's red hair was revealed when he took off
the SWAT black baseball cap and scratched his head.
And he laughed, gold teeth glinting in the moonlight.

"Right, Luther. So, don't keep a civil tongue in your head. Whatchya doin'?"

"Want a lift out to the islands."

"Plannin' on a little vacation? Hear it's lovely this time of year."

"It is," Holden interjected.

Loman looked at him, then at Steel. "Then the rumors I been hearin' are true. There is a deal between the director and the Patriots."

"Where'd you hear a silly thing like that?" Luther Steel smiled.

"Oh, hell, I don't remember. Maybe in a secret Justice Department memo to the House Committee on Domestic Violence and House Speaker Roman Makowski. Maybe I saw it written on the wall of some phone booth. Get to be fiftyish like me, hell, the memory goes first. The dick works great and the legs are good, but the memory— what was I talkin' about anyway?" He shook Luther Steel's hand, then offered his hand to Holden.

Holden took it.

CHAPTER

2

It was not the ideal night for what they had planned. The moon was nearly bright enough that David Holden could read the emergency safety precautions stenciled over the helicopter's open doorway beside which he sat. The heightening of the wind made it bone chillingly cold over the tossing white caps, despite the oppressive heat of the afternoon before the sun had dropped away. The wind rushed through the gunship laterally as if the ship were merely a short wind tunnel. Like the other men in the chopper, but for different reasons, Holden's head and face and throat were masked with a black, skin-tight hood, broken only by eyeholes and a mouthhole. Even with the hood and his black leather gloves and the M-65 field jacket's collar turned up, he was still cold. He would have wondered if one of his wounds had turned septic, causing him to have a fever, but Luther Steel and the Special Operations Group personnel seemed just as uncomfortable. The velocity of the air currents would make the rapelling operation, the first element the assembled Special Operations Groups would utilize for insertion,

more than usually dangerous. It was already dangerous
enough.

Biff Loman stood at the center of the fuselage between
the two open doors. Three men on each side in black
webbing Swiss seats, heavily gloved fists balled to the
ropes wound round their subdued steel descenders. They
planned a fast descent, and no one controlled it but themselves. If the descent rate went out of control, death or
crippling injury would result.

Holden's palms sweated inside his gloves—and he
wasn't even jumping. He'd done it in the SEALs, been
scared to death that first time and only mildly terrified
after that. Being mildly terrified nurtured the proper respect for the situation and kept you alive. Hotshoting led
to accidents, for the careless man and the ones around
him. Even the simplest rapell was dangerous, even the
best rope could break, even the most trained man could
lose his cool and go into freefall. Swinging in the wind
like a marionette beneath a hovering helicopter while enemy fire might be directed at you from below was beyond
unnerving.

Biff Loman ran a last-minute equipment check. Descenders and carabiners, already checked a dozen times,
were checked again; special thick black leather gloves designed to guard against rope burn were tugged just once
more; M-16 and Heckler & Koch submachine gun slings
checked for tightness; the men's SAS-style holsters were
verified for proper closure. Holden recognized these holsters; they were identical to the one in which he carried
the Desert Eagle Rufus Burroughs had used, but these
Southwind Sanctions SAS holsters carried 9mm Sig-
Sauer P-226s instead of outsized Israeli .44 Magnum
semiautomatic pistols.

The pilot of the gunship shouted, "In position, Agent Loman! We're over the drop zone now."

"Gotchya!" Loman looked from side to side as he addressed the men of his team. "We want those FLNA bastards alive if we can, but we want the hostages and you guys alive more. Right?" Some three hundred presumably innocent and uninvolved registered guests were still present at the Cedar Ridge Islands complex, hopefully still alive. A chorus of affirmations sounded from the Special Operations Group personnel. There was no estimate, however speculative, as to how many FLNA people were on the islands, and although each man didn't know exactly what he faced, he knew death was a distinct possibility. Loman grabbed up the seventh rope, quickly and surely locking on, as one of the men checked his equipment.

"Let's move!" Loman stepped out onto the runner. His men did the same, and the ropes suddenly became taut. The helicopter swayed slightly, as if out of balance for an instant. "Hit it!" Holden heard Loman shout. Then Loman jumped. The next instant his six-man team flew after him. The gunship's frame vibrated briefly with a sudden lurch as weight shifted dramatically.

They were gone.

Luther Steel, clipped on to a safety line, leaned toward the edge of an open door. Holden, also clipped to a safety line, dropped into a crouch beside him. Like tracer fire—and perhaps some rounds were indeed tracers—streaks of light zigzagged crazily through the darkness below them. Flares were fired. Heavy automatic weapons fire was angling upward toward the downward-rapelling men and toward the helicopters from which they dropped. Holden tucked back. Steel did the same as bullets whined off the runners below them and off the fuselage itself. One of the

rapelling men slid downward too fast along the length of
his rope, nearly to the ground, then hung there like a
crippled marionette, swaying. Others from the team were
on the ground, returning fire. One of the team—it had to
be Loman himself because of his size—ran to the injured
man. The flash of a blade was visible in the glow of a
bursting ground flare, then the injured or dead SOG man
was cut off his belay, slung over a shoulder, taken to
cover.

"Those poor guys are sitting ducks!" Steel shouted
over the keening wind and the all-pervasive cacophony of
the rotor blades' downdraft and the whining ricochets of
bullets. Steel shoved his assault rifle through the opening,
then slammed it down across his thighs in a gesture of
futility. In the darkness below them, darkness punctuated
only by the occasional flare or the flash of an explosion,
any gunfire directed downward, if it hit anyone at all,
might just as easily harm the growing number of Special
Operations Group personnel descending from the helicopters around them.

David Holden, unclipped from his safety line, was already starting forward to the helicopter pilot.

"I've got an all-clear from the ground," the pilot
called, turning to look up at him. "I'll be pulling off
shore."

Holden drew the Desert Eagle from the Southwind
holster at his right thigh. "No, you won't. Get us in
there. Now!"

The pilot looked toward the muzzle of the black .44
Magnum autoloader. "But—"

"Now! Then you clear out. Take her down! We'll need
ten seconds at touchdown, then boogie."

The pilot licked his lips, his face pale. He nodded, the
machine lurching under Holden's booted feet as it slipped

to port and began to bank slightly. Holden stayed beside the pilot, and Steel suddenly appeared there.

"What are you doing?"

"The pilot volunteered to take us in. Be ready to jump when he's skimming the ground. We'll have ten seconds for egress. It'll be the best chance we'll get," Holden said.

Steel's eyes were pinpoints of almost black light, the green glow of the overhead from the cockpit flickering in them, giving them a look of amusement or something less definable. But then he nodded, starting to unlimber his M-16.

"You can take the gun off me. I'm goin' in already," the pilot shouted to Holden.

Holden looked at him, then holstered his gun, securing the safety strap as he gave the man a thumbs-up.

David Holden walked back toward the starboard side door, standing just inside the opening opposite Luther Steel. If anything, the volume of gunfire from below had increased now, and the explosions—they sounded like grenades—were more frequent; but the hits against the helicopter itself had ceased. Evidently a fast-moving target was beyond the abilities of the FLNA marksmen on the ground.

The helicopter veered over the foaming whitecaps, spray blowing against their faces and masks and soaking their clothing and equipment. The guns would need a good cleaning and quickly, Holden mentally noted. Salt spray's corrosive effect was like a cancer to metal.

Steel held the M-16 by the front stock. Holden swung the MP5 SD3 forward on its sling. The helicopter skimmed over the rocks beyond the low seawall to the landing pad. Rosie had been packed aboard the Cedar Ridge Islands commuter chopper there, preparatory to being thrown to her death. Holden had jumped aboard the helicopter, fought with Borsoi/Johnson there. And the Soviet agent provocateur who led the FLNA in Metro and who might be its overall field commander had fallen from the helicopter into the inky blackness of the Atlantic. It seemed forever ago, but was only a few nights ago.

At least Borsoi/Johnson was dead.

They were over one of the fairways now, circling back, slipping to the helipad. Then the pilot shouted, "Touchdown!"

Luther Steel, his voice a bizarre mixture of laughter and terror, shouted, "Hike!" He jumped into the night, Holden beside him. Gunfire was everywhere around them. The helicopter slipped away and upward, rotating a full 180 degrees on its axis as Holden and Steel ran to what cover there was—an overturned golf cart with a knot of Special Operations Group personnel crouched behind it.

Bullets *pinged* off the cart's bodywork, chunks of metal ripping away.

"Where are they?"

"Behind that other golf cart, Steel!" Loman shouted back. "Three of 'em, anyway."

Holden shot a glance around the side of the cart and tucked back a split second before a fusillade of gunfire— assault rifle fire—tore into the cart. If he hadn't known by the sound and intensity, he would have known by the effect—an entire chunk of the upended cart's left rear fender was shot away. Rifle bullets did that, not handgun bullets, not usually.

Holden rocked back on his haunches. "If they're smart, they know how many of us there are. If they're smart, they know what our guns can do. But I don't think they're that smart. Count of five, everybody spray out assault rifles and subguns into the golf cart. If we get 'em, terrific. If we don't, I'll get them."

Loman's eyes just peered at him from behind the mask, visible for an instant in the flash of light from an explosion. "You nuts or you got a plan?"

"Maybe a little of both."

"Listen to him," Steel prompted.

"Start countin'." Loman nodded.

Holden shoved the H&K submachine gun into his left fist as he counted, "One . . . two . . . three . . . four . . . FIVE!" He dodged left, with Luther Steel behind and slightly above him. Hot brass sprayed Holden from both sides and from above as he fired out his submachine gun into the golf cart fifty or sixty yards away. Trailers of sparks flew in all directions as bullets whined off the cart.

As Holden and the others emptied their guns, they pulled back. Immediately there was a heavy volume of answering fire. Holden pushed the H&K and a spare magazine for it into Steel's hands, threw himself prone in the wet grass behind the cart, and stabbed the Desert Eagle through a shot-out portion of the cart where they were taking cover. He worked the safety as he settled the muzzle, then began to fire. The Desert Eagle's sudden roar drowned out the sounds of the others reloading. The bright orange tongues of flame licking from the Desert Eagle's muzzle were blindingly bright. Holden kept firing, emptying the pistol's eight-round magazine as he zigzagged the muzzle from left to right and started it back.

"Charge them now!" Holden shouted, stuffing the empty Desert Eagle into the front of his pistol belt as he rose to a crouch and grabbed the H&K submachine gun from Steel's hands. Holden, Steel, Loman, and the SOG personnel ran from both sides of the golf cart, closing on the enemy position. The volume of answering fire was almost negligible.

Holden was the second man to reach the far side of the cart where the FLNA personnel had taken cover. A man, already wounded, stabbed an assault rifle toward him, but Holden fired first, stitching a half-dozen 9mm parabellums across the FLNA-er's chest, throat, and face.

Steel was dispatching another one, two quick bursts from the M-16 in his fists. A flare burst, and in its yellow glow Holden saw the gaping ragged holes in the metal of the golf cart's body, not long runs of holes made by the SOG unit's assault rifles, but single holes, wider. The slugs from the Desert Eagle.

Loman was shouting, "Along that fairway toward the inn! Follow me!" Gunfire was coming from the trees. Some of the SOG personnel were going down, others returning fire or hurtling grenades as they charged ahead.

Holden shouted to Luther Steel, "Come on!" As Holden ran, his wounds chipping away at his resolve, he rammed a fresh magazine up the well of the Desert Eagle and pocketed the empty.

Rosie Shepherd had told him every detail of her capture and subsequent confinement beneath the executive suite of the inn. She had described a tunnel leading to the room in which she'd been held—if he were the FLNA leadership on Cedar Ridge Islands, that was where he would hide. Rescuing hostages was the job of the Special Operations Group personnel. He and Luther Steel had come for something else: information. And, perhaps, killing.

As he recognized his own thoughts, something went through his stomach, churning inside him, making the cold sweat return. What had he become? He knew why,

though. The faces of his wife and his children, of Rufus
Burroughs, of Burroughs's wife Annette, of all the other
innocent dead—all appeared before him.

No court.

No swap for diplomatic reasons.

If Charlie Lang and some of the other FLNA leadership remained on the island, as logic dictated they had to
have, killing them would bring the end of things that
much quicker. And if murder on his hands and in his
soul would save other innocent lives, then murder it
would be. He kept running, slipping once on the grass.
Steel was right beside him now. Holden's entire being
was consumed with the pain of his wounds, but his legs
were still pumping. The inn's gradually clearer black and
gray shadow was before him; no lights were lit. What
kind of terror had the well-to-do guests of Cedar Ridge
Islands, the poor who were their waitresses and busboys
and maids, the uninvolved members of the staff—what
kind of terror had they endured? Even now, were some of
them being put to death out of sheer spite, sheer evil?

A grenade fell near them and Holden heard Steel shout
something. As he threw himself to the ground, chunks of
turf from the manicured greens of the golf course hurtling over them, Holden was glad for the face mask and
the protection, however meager, it afforded.

"All right?" he shouted toward Steel.

Already the FBI man was starting shakily to his feet.

Holden stood and almost fell, a wave of pain from his
leg washing over him. He threw himself back into the
run, the Desert Eagle in one fist, the H&K submachine
gun in the other.

The ground began to rise suddenly, sharply. Holden
leaned into it as he ran on, his lungs aching with the

exertion. Steel, outdistancing him, reached the low stone
wall that surrounded the inn's main building first and
flattened himself against it. The sounds of battle were
mainly to their right. Most of the Special Operations
Group were by the breech in the wall, closing on the
driveways that led toward the main entrance.

Suddenly the sound of helicopters filled the air. Holden
hit the wall and sagged against it, looking up. "The second prong of the attack!" Steel shouted, breathless.

Helicopters, but gunships this time, were approaching
from the west, spaced wide apart but coming in a straight
line.

As the first of them came near to the wall, rapelling
lines were dropped. The helicopters angled downward
and men appeared on the lines. Steel shouted, "U.S. Marshal Service Special Operations Group. They train near
here!" The helicopters leveled off and, simultaneously,
the marshals started to descend. They swung down into
the yard beyond the wall almost as rapidly as if their
descents were uncontrolled. Holden watched them as he
climbed, exposing himself there on the top of the wall as
he stared unconsciously. It was the slickest operation
he'd ever seen.

The first element was down, the gunship swept away to
the north as the second element began their descent. Already the marshals from the first group were storming
the front of the inn. They wore dark-blue coveralls and
full riot gear. Gas grenades fired as they were hurtled
through shot-out windows. The Marshals burst through
ground-level windows and the doorway proper, M-16s
and riot shotguns at high port.

Now Steel was over the wall. Holden jumped after

him, coming down hard. His leg gave way but he caught himself.

Holden veered left, limping badly now, moving toward the seemingly erratically boarded-up side windows facing the runwaylike apron of concrete that ran the full length of the inn from the main doors. Steel was beside and just a little ahead of him. The building seemed to shimmer as an explosion rocked outward. The boards over the windows splintered, sending shards of glass the size of Bowie knives hurtling everywhere. Holden dove to the ground and the meager cover of a hedgerow. Steel shouted something, but the words were drowned out in the noise of the explosion.

Holden's ears rang as he pushed himself up. Glass tinkled from his back and shoulders and legs, crunched under his booted feet as he drew himself up into a crouch. Fire belched from the openings where windows had been an instant before.

Steel was to his feet. In the firelight a bloodstain was visible on his left thigh. "Just a scratch—a big one, but a scratch. Glass," Steel shouted, answering Holden's unasked question.

Anyone inside the building near the explosion—hostages, FLNA, men from the Marshal Service or any of the other Justice Department personnel—would have been killed, Holden realized. Flames licked skyward now through a gaping hole in the roof. Holden edged back, looking up. The night was tinged with red and flickering gold.

He licked his lips, tasting the fabric of his mask. It tasted like sweat to him, sweat and fear. He shook off the sensation, then signaled to Steel as he moved along the side of the building. His heart beat so rapidly he felt it pounding. Was there another explosion waiting to be detonated? They kept moving and reached an employee entrance. The door was open. Men in business suits, sports clothes, even shorts were running from the building, all of them armed with M-16s, Uzis, and handguns.

"FLNA!" Steel shouted.

Some of the fleeing men wheeled toward them, opening fire. Holden opened fire, and Steel's M-16 spat death as well. FLNA-ers went down. Half a dozen made a run into the trees near the wall, the rest disappeared back inside.

Holden, unscathed, assumed Steel was too as he moved to a flanking position beside the doorway, spraying his H&K submachine gun toward the FLNA-ers near the wall. Sporadic gunfire was returned, but they were more interested in fleeing than fighting, Holden realized. Steel was changing sticks for his M-16. Holden reached to his web gear.

"Sound and light!" he shouted. Steel nodded as Holden tore the grenade from the harness, simultaneously ripping the pin. He hurled it through the acrid-smelling smoke billowing out from the open doorway, then averted his eyes and covered his ears with his hands. Much of the light effect would be diminished by the smoke, but the sound's stunning effect might be enough to buy the few seconds they needed to get inside.

The grenade's whistling sound was insanely loud, even considering the distance to its detonation point and that his ears were covered. As the dopplerlike effect of the sound waned, Holden signaled to Steel. Steel nodded, the black FBI Agent's right fist on the pistol grip of his M-16, his left fist clenched on the butt of his Sig-Sauer P-226, one of the twenty-round extension magazines in place.

As Holden whacked a fresh magazine home in the

MP5 SD3, he dodged right to left through the doorway, a blur of motion as Steel dodged left to right.

In the flickering of the firelight, human bodies could be seen everywhere. Burning pieces of garbage, chunks of ceiling tile, fiery bits of broken furniture were strewn around them. Throats were slit ear to ear on some of the bodies, on others bullet wounds visible to the heads and necks. The flesh of some was gray; others were still pink with life. Systematic murder. The FLNA-ers from the doorway had dispersed, some of them staggering blindly through the smoke, hands over their ears, others who knew where. Holden opened fire. Steel, beside him, did the same, cutting down the remaining FLNA-ers. One of the men who'd been wearing shorts opened fire blindly with his Uzi. Steel put two bursts into his abdomen and chest. Two more of the men, their business suits tattered and dirty, were firing from behind an overturned sofa. After Holden hosed the H&K into the seat of the sofa and through, both men tumbled down from behind it, dead. As to the others—Holden aimed the larger of the two Berettas and fired a shot in the left temple of a man in gray suit pants and vest, his tie stupidly still at full mast but hanging outside the vest; a double tap into the gaping mouth of an FLNA-er raising his Uzi to fire; two rounds, then two more into the chest and neck of an FLNA-er charging toward them blindly with a chair-leg club in his upraised right fist. They were all down, dead. Holden holstered the partially spent Beretta, then, as he put a fresh magazine up the butt of the H&K, bent to one of the nearer bodies and picked up an Uzi dropped by one of the dead FLNA-ers, then another, slinging both off his left shoulder. Steel, his Sig-Sauer 9mm stuffed into his belt, picked up a second M-16.

Both men buttoned out the magazines already in the

weapons, found fresh ones among the bodies, and reloaded.

"Which way to that office you were telling me about?"

Holden looked at Luther Steel, then nodded toward where the smoke seemed least dense and the long, wood-paneled corridor beyond it. They started moving.

CHAPTER
3

Charlie Lang held the machine gun or submachine gun or whatever it was in his left hand. Holding a gun was as awkward and unnatural to him as holding a broom. His hands—graceful hands, his mother had always called them—were meant to hold a pen, to take the written word and turn it into art. He moved along in the wake of the five FLNA section commanders. They were surrounded by an entourage of frightened women—waitresses in ragged ankle-length Victorian domestic uniforms with smoke- and dirt-splotched white aprons, almost as dirty as their faces; wealthy women patrons of Cedar Ridge Islands, most dressed in tennis or golf clothes, but equally dirty; some older female children. There were eighteen in all, kept in a ragged formation around the five section commanders and Charlie Lang himself.

What the hell had happened to Borsoi? Charlie Lang almost asked. And Borsoi's record book. He had told the man never to take it with him, to memorize the names; but, intelligent as he was, Borsoi was poor at memorization and—Lang had known that from the start—vastly overconfident. What had happened to him? Why was a blockade cutting off the islands?

"Keep moving! Quickly!" It was Muli who spoke, the one the other four section commanders seemed afraid of. Lang feared him too. Muli was fresh from Lebanon, he knew, and was so widely sought by police that he'd had his face changed with plastic surgery. No surgeon could have altered the black hatred that burned in Muli's eyes. A little girl tripped—she couldn't have been more than fourteen—and Lang impulsively started to reach out to help her. Muli pushed the butt of his rifle into her right kidney and she screamed, then he kicked her repeatedly until she stood up and struggled on. Her mother tried to protect her and at the same time keep from dropping the box of files she carried. The girl had spilled her files across the stone floor. Muli kicked her again as she struggled to pick them up, sending her sprawling. All the women were carrying boxes and large manila envelopes stuffed with data on FLNA operations throughout the United States, Mexico, and Canada. Muli kicked her again. At last, her lips bleeding profusely, she had the files clutched against her breasts and struggled ahead. Muli caught up his can of gasoline and went on. The smell of the two-gallon gasoline cans—each of the five section commanders carried one—was overpoweringly strong there.

It was cold too in the damp tunnel leading from Lang's office toward the storage rooms and maybe, if the chaos above them continued long enough, leading to a chance at escape. Three launches had been prepared for escape when it was realized that Cedar Ridge Islands was cut off from the mainland, cut off by air and sea, cut off from any hope of being reached by one of the Soviet vessels that brought in the foreign nationals who became section commanders—like Muli and the four others.

The power on the islands had been cut hours before. The emergency generators Cedar Ridge Islands maintained for the comfort of its guests had tripped on automatically, but they provided emergency lighting and air conditioning for only a few rooms. With no fresh air being pumped in, the dampness of the tunnel was turning to sweat on the walls and on the ceiling itself. Charlie Lang touched at his perfectly cut, now-disarrayed white hair. His hair had always been a source of pride to him. In prison he had been forced to keep it short, not been allowed the hot-oil treatments for his scalp. He'd felt it noticeably thinning.

He blotted moisture away from his forehead with his once-white handkerchief—perspiration? Or more of the damned condensation dripping off the ceiling?

They neared the end of the tunnel.

Beyond it he could see the racks of clothing for the next batch of men who came off the trawler or the submarine. The clothing would be burned now. They were cheap things, but distinctively American. Everything was aimed at making men like Muli and the others blend in, reach their assignments surreptitiously, inconspicuously.

"Put them down now!" Muli commanded the women to throw down their burdens.

The clothing, the files, all of it—but not— "No!"

"Silence if you wish to escape with us, old man!" Muli stabbed the knife that had suddenly appeared in his hand into the abdomen of one of the waitresses. Blood spurted all over her apron as she screamed and fell. Now there was screaming everywhere. Muli was hacking at another woman amid gunfire as the other four opened fire on the hostages. Lang dropped his gun and held his hands over his ears, his eyes squeezed tight against what was happening, his face and hands feeling the spattering of blood, the screaming so loud he could not blot it from his mind.

And then, the smell of gasoline.

He opened his eyes.

Muli was pouring out the contents of his two-gallon gasoline cannister across the body of the first woman he had killed, over the files beneath her body. The other section commanders were throwing clothing down from the racks, burying the women's bodies under sport coats and slacks and raincoats and more files, then pouring on more gasoline.

Charlie Lang reached down to the floor for his gun and drew his hand back. His gun was blood-splattered. He stepped away from it hurriedly as he rose, slipping, almost losing his balance. He looked to the floor beneath his feet. It was slick with gradually expanding gouts of blood.

Lang began to weep.

"Here! Hold this!" Muli handed Lang his gun. Lang almost dropped it. Muli took a disposable lighter from the pocket of his trousers and fired it, catching up a sheaf of driver's license blanks, setting them afire. He fanned the papers, making the flames heighten, then tossed the improvised torch onto the body of one of the waitresses. Her gasoline-soaked skirts caught fire immediately.

"Butcher!"

Lang wasn't conscious of saying the word.

Muli took the gun from him, laughed, then shoved him forward. Lang almost lost his footing again; he slipped to his knees finally, the flames licking toward the ceiling now, the smell of burning flesh making him vomit all over his trousers. Muli shoved him ahead.

Lang coughed up more vomit and tried to stand.

CHAPTER
4

David Holden smelled smoke from ahead, an overpowering smell of gasoline and something else, sweet, putrid. Luther Steel ripped away his face mask. Holden did the same. "Oh, my God," Steel rasped.

Holden inhaled, chills traveling along his spine and up both sides of his neck and across the top of his head. His body was trembling. He ran as fast as he could along the tunnel now, his weapons shifted so that one of the captured Uzis was slung to each shoulder, the H&K submachine gun still slung at his right side to be used when the Uzis were spent and discarded.

Steel crowded beside him, running full out. The pain in Holden's leg was still there, still gnawing at him, his leg damp with blood from the reopened wound. He kept running, the pain only there like a ghost, not something real that could stop him.

They rounded a right-angle bend in the tunnel. Ahead, in the distance, Holden could see the glow of flames. The gasoline smell grew stronger. And the other smell.

Holden threw his body into a run, more a continuous lunge now than any sort of pace, hurling himself along the tunnel, Steel matching him stride for stride. Sweat dripped into Holden's eyes and he wiped it away. Steel's face glistened with it.

Holden crossed out of the tunnel into a large room. Empty clothing racks littered the walls, and a huge bonfire roared immediately in front of him. The body of a woman—no more than a girl—suddenly rose out of the flames at the near edge of the fire. Steel screamed.

She lurched toward them, something like a moan coming from the flames. She was a living torch, hair and face and clothing consumed by flames, her hands black as they waved toward him, then clasped together in a gesture of prayer.

David Holden wretched as he fell to his knees. Summoning up every ounce of his strength, his weapons suddenly impossibly heavy in his hands, he fired both submachine guns into her. As her body sprawled back, mercifully dead, Steel gasped. "Look!"

Still on his knees, David Holden wheeled the muzzles of the weapons toward the bonfire itself. There were bodies everywhere, some of them still moving, all of them living dead. Holden fired. Steel raised an assault rifle as if in slow motion, then sprayed it out into the flames. When it was empty, he threw it down and grabbed up the second one. Holden let both expropriated submachine guns fall from his hands. He swung his own forward with his right hand, his left hand grasping the butt of the already partially spent pistol in his belt.

Gunfire reverberated from the walls around them. Hot brass pelted his exposed face and neck until he could no longer feel it.

His guns were empty.

Steel was repeatedly clicking the automatic pistol in his left hand, but the gun was empty. Somehow he had

worked the slide release and he was simply double action-
ing it.

Tears streamed down Steel's cheeks.

Holden vomited again.

"Motherfuckers!" Steel sobbed.

David Holden, his eyes washed with tears, rammed a
fresh magazine up the butt of his submachine gun. The
pistol he had fired lay empty on the floor beside him.

He picked it up, wiped the vomit from the slide against
his left thigh, and reloaded it. Holden let the slide run
forward over a twenty-round magazine, worked the
safety down to drop the hammer, and rammed it into his
waistband. Then he stood, his knees blood-slicked.

Luther Steel reloaded the one assault rifle he still held,
then his pistol.

Neither man spoke.

They both started to run.

CHAPTER
5

Charlie Lang shivered as the night wind hit him. The entrance to the underground area beneath the inn was shrouded by natural foliage, which had served as a windbreak. Now they were on clear ground.

His hands were sticky and he didn't want to remember with what.

Muli was running ahead, toward the nearest of the boats. Lang tried to force himself to keep up.

Would they kill him? Were they taking him along just to kill him? All the details in the burned files were still somewhere in his brain. Or did they need those details, were they keeping him alive just for that?

He quickened his pace, his heart pounding in his chest. But, he told himself, that was terror.

All those women.

Tears streamed down his cheeks again at the remembrance of the sight. His throat felt tight. He tore at his collar to open it, but it was already open. He tried to run, for Muli and two of the others were already at the boat dock.

They'd never get away. He could give himself up. The

American authorities were that way, not vindictive. If he offered voluntary evidence, told about the dozens of other Roger Costigans who were superpatriots on the outside but were bought and paid for by the FLNA and the FLNA's masters, the government would treat him well, put him someplace nice under protective custody.

He could demand the best treatment and get it, just by giving them only a little information at a time.

But the thing in the corridor underground.

He could say he knew nothing about that. They couldn't read the nightmares he would have forever seeing it, feeling it. He could angle off now, away from the boats, surrender to some of the invading Justice Department forces.

They would know how valuable he was, had probably memorized his face.

The remaining two section commanders had joined Muli at the dock. Now all five were hovering around the boats.

Charlie Lang stopped in his tracks, hearing a shout from behind him.

What had the voice proclaimed? It wasn't "Stop! You are under arrest!" It was—he heard it again now. "Die, you rotten bastards!"

Charlie Lang turned around so quickly, his hands already raising, that he almost lost his balance. Two men, running from the entrance to the underground tunnel, came out of the trees. In the moonlight he could see them clearly. Both wore black, both had weapons, both were big men, tall, well set in the shoulders. One of them was black, the other white, a shock of dark curly hair on his head.

The black man was suddenly on him. Lang felt the life

drain out of him as a rifle butt impacted him in the chest and he fell back.

The white man jumped over him.

Lang rolled onto his stomach, his eyes following the two men as they charged toward the boats.

Muli and the other four section commanders opened fire, as did the two men. One of the section commanders was down. The black man was hit, fell, his left hand to his left shoulder, his right hand still firing his weapon. Tongues of flame licked into the blackness. Lang could hardly breathe from the pain in his chest where the rifle butt had struck him. But he couldn't close his eyes.

Now the black man was up, running toward the boats again, still firing. Another of the section commanders went down as the white man with the curly hair fired again. One of the boats was clearing the docks. The black man and the white man fired on it. And suddenly the boat just wasn't there. A huge fireball of black and yellow lit the sky, and the same sickening smell of gasoline Lang had smelled in the tunnel washed into the air. Pieces of the boat were aflame on the water.

Muli was in the prow of another boat. He stabbed his gun toward the white man who was nearest to him, fired, but only a few shots. Then Muli threw down the gun and in the firelight there was the flash of his knife. Lang imagined it still slick with the blood of the first woman who'd been killed.

The white man jumped down into the boat. The burning vessel backlit them. The man with the curly hair drew a knife from beneath his right shoulder, the glint of polished steel catching the firelight.

The black man shouted, "Let me kill him, David!"

The white man with the curly hair—David—shouted

up to him where he stood legs wide apart, a weapon in each hand at the edge of the dock, "No!"

And then the curly-haired one—David—lunged. Muli backstepped. The sound of steel against steel was barely audible over the crackle of flames, the rush of the wind, and the lap of the surf.

Muli and the curly-haired man were locked in combat, arms over their heads, their steel glinting in the firelight. The curly-haired man fell back. Muli dove for him as David shouted, "Don't kill him, Luther!" Then David rolled aside as Muli impacted the boat's gunwale. The sound of steel against steel rang out again as their blades locked.

David's left fist flashed out, rocking Muli's head back. Muli countered with his knife. David jumped back and seemed to lose his balance for a moment, but he was well out of the way of the knife. As Muli recovered, lunged, thrust with his knife, David vaulted to one side, his legs sweeping out and knocking Muli off his feet.

As Muli started to rise, the curly-haired man was on him, his blade flashing in the firelight. A scream came from Muli—it was like the screams of the dying women —and something flew away from his body. The knife— but something else, little things. "Ohh—" Lang choked on his breath. They were Muli's fingers.

He heard David shout as the knife in his hand rose, then hammered downward. The man shouted, "Die, you bag of shit!"

Charlie Lang screamed because of where David stabbed Muli: The knife was buried in Muli's face.

CHAPTER

6

The black man showed him an identity card inside a folding leather badge case.

"Charles Whittington Lang." As the tall black man rolled him over onto his stomach again, Lang suddenly felt the familiar, oddly almost comforting sensations as the bracelets were clamped over his wrists. "I am Special Agent Steel with the Federal Bureau of Investigation. I have a federal warrant for your arrest on multiple charges of treason and subversion, complicity to felony homicides, and various other charges. You have the right to remain silent. Anything you say can and will be used against you in a court of law. You have the right to an attorney . . ."

When he concluded the litany, Charlie Lang said, "I'll cooperate. I'll tell you anything. I want to make a deal."

"I am not at liberty to discuss such matters with you, but I'll relay your remarks to the proper persons." He stood over Lang, patted him down expertly, and now was searching his pockets.

"I don't have a gun. They made me carry one for a

while but I dropped it. They were evil men, Agent—
Steel, is it?"

"Steel."

"They were evil men. I tried to stop them. I tried
so—"

And then the black FBI man rolled him onto his back
and hauled him to his feet. Charlie Lang was suddenly
terrified. The man had a pistol in his right hand. And the
gun was vibrating just like Charlie Lang's body trembled.
Agent Steel's eyes were like glowing black coals and his
teeth were gritted together so that the tendons in his neck
vibrated like the gun. Charlie Lang's eyes went back to
the gun. "Look, you vile cocksucker," Steel said in a soft,
menacing tone. "I enforce the law. I'm not supposed to
execute people. And just maybe the information in your
head's important enough that they won't give you the
death penalty. God knows you deserve worse. But don't
push me, or you'll be just one more casualty. So help me
God you will."

To Lang, Agent Steel seemed somehow more lethal
than Muli or any of the others ever had. And Charlie
Lang wet his pants.

CHAPTER
7

David Holden had slipped back to the mainland along with a mixed group of Justice Department Special Operations Group personnel. Because of the fast action by the Marshal Service personnel who had assaulted the inn itself, only the hostages who had been killed in the initial bomb blast and those he and Steel had found incinerated in the underground complex had died. The other 218 hostages were rescued, along with the remainder of the imprisoned Cedar Ridge Islands staff.

The combined Justice Department personnel had killed or captured seventy-nine identifiable FLNA-ers. Another few dozen persons found on the islands were being interrogated to determine whether they should be held for further questioning or released to debriefing.

Holden slipped away, removing his mask as he limped along the shoreline to the north of the staging area. He paused, closing his coat over his gunbelt. It looked bulky but in the gray light before dawn, he wouldn't be immediately recognizable as armed. He unbloused his combat boots, letting the BDU pants fall over them to his ankles. The submachine gun had been borrowed, and he'd left it with Steel after the fight on the boat. The rest of the fighting had stopped by then.

Holden undid the buckle that held the Southwind Sanctions holster for the Desert Eagle to his belt. He extracted the .44 autoloader, raised the front of his jacket and thrust the gun into his belt beneath, then folded the black fabric holster around the spare magazine it held and stuffed this inside his jacket.

He looked like a bumpy fat man, he thought, but there was no humor in him.

He kept walking, letting the surf lap up over his boots to wash away some of the blood.

In the distance he saw the car.

What would he tell Rosie Shepherd? Nothing? She was tough. He thought he had been toughened by the events that had changed so dramatically everything in his life, by the deaths of his family, by all the dying since. But nothing had toughened him enough.

It was an FOUO car, and he supposed one could look on this as official use. Rosie and FBI Agent Clark Pietrowski, one of Luther Steel's special squad, were waiting to pick him up.

He should have listened to Rosie, shouldn't have gone to Cedar Ridge Islands. He should have listened. His trouser leg was wet with blood, much of it his own from the reopened wound.

He wondered how many yards it was until he reached the car. Usually he would have known.

David Holden stopped walking and dropped to his knees in the surf. He began to cry.

Rose Shepherd said to Clark Pietrowski, "That's gotta be David. He's wounded!" She shoved open the Ford's passenger door and ran, her track shoes digging into the sand, already filling with it. Old Clark Pietrowski, behind her, was shouting, "Watch out in case it isn't—" But she could no longer hear him. Her purse was over her shoulder and she had the flap opened as she ran. She grabbed the Detonics Servicemaster .45 from inside and jacked back the hammer with her thumb.

It was David.

She slowed a little, calling out to him. "David?"

He was just kneeling there in the water.

She ran ahead, her eyes shifting up and down the length of the beach. What was wrong?

Rose Shepherd skidded into the sand beside him on her blue-jeaned knees, reached out to touch— "Don't touch me," David hissed. "I'm covered with blood. Just don't. Don't."

Rose Shepherd stayed there on her knees beside him, wanting to touch him very much.

Clark Pietrowski walked up. She could see his shoes in the sand beside her. They were wingtips like her father would sometimes wear with his good suit when he was off duty from the cops. A flashlight beam washed across David's face, illuminating the tears in his eyes. The flashlight beam swept down the length of his body as far as possible. His clothing was covered with blood.

"Professor Holden? What the—"

"Leave it alone, Pietrowski."

"What—"

"Women and girls. A dozen or more at least. They burned them. Some of them were alive. So leave it alone."

Rose Shepherd reached out to him, and David Holden stood up and moved away. "I'm dirty. With blood. Don't touch me now," David said, not looking at her. "Not now. Not until I wash it away. Not now." And he started to walk into the surf.

She stood there for a minute, just watching him. He was in the water up to his thighs before she could think of what to do, then he was in up to his waist.

Clark Pietrowski stirred beside her and, as she turned her head to look at him, she saw him flip the D-cell police flashlight in his left hand. He was into the water in three strides, beside David in three or four more. Before she could react, the butt of the flashlight flicked outward against David's neck.

She started to scream; she'd never been a screamer. She didn't scream out a warning, though.

"Help me with him, Rosie; he's been through some heavy shit," Pietrowski called over the lapping of the surf, barely audible as he caught David in his arms and started dragging him out of the water. Rose ran to help.

She had cleaned the Desert Eagle first, since its disassembly procedure was the least familiar to her of David's guns. Then the small Beretta 92F Compact—it appeared not to have been fired at all—and then the full-sized military Beretta. That had been fired a lot.

She cleaned the knife too. Inscribed on the blade were the words "The Defender." She scrubbed at it with the toothbrush from the cleaning kit because there was blood caked in the lettering.

There was a doctor in with David, one Clark Pietrowski had gotten. David's leg wound had opened up. But that was the least of her worries.

Rose Shepherd had seen his eyes. His eyes—or what was behind them—worried her.

She fought back her own tears. At least Borsoi was dead, and although it would be naive to assume that the FLNA was crushed, what had happened on Cedar Ridge Islands combined with Borsoi's having perished had to have seriously confounded their timetable, cost them critical personnel and leadership. Clark Pietrowski had said that Charlie Lang was taken alive but all the records were destroyed. There was an odd look in his eyes when he said that. But if Lang had kept the FLNA records, perhaps there was enough still in his head, coupled with the record books taken from Costigan and Borsoi, to crack the FLNA organization wide open.

Maybe.

She kept scrubbing, the caked blood coming out of the engraving on the blade of David's knife at last. But whatever he had seen there, how long would it take for the horror of it to leave his soul?

Maybe with time all of this would come to an end. Life would return to normal, and she could just be with David in some happy place.

Rose Shepherd could no longer read the lettering on the Crain knife in her hands, her vision too blurred with tears.

And where was there a happy place? She had read about them in books, and sometimes other people traveled there. But it had to be a private club—the happy place—and she had been born without a membership card.

So had David.

CHAPTER
8

Dimitri Borsoi was uncomfortable in the Ford's front passenger seat, but sitting there was his only option. It would not be good to show himself so vulnerable, so weakened before the Leopards. Not good at all.

They knew that he had been injured—that much would be evident to even the dimmest-witted among them by the bruises on his face and hands. The bruises beneath his clothing and the fractures in his legs were another matter. The bruises across his chest, shoulders, and thighs were seen only by those who attended him, though his arms moved stiffly still. The casts over his legs were specially molded by an FLNA sympathizer doctor so that, under normal suit pants, they would not be seen readily. He had broken both shins and one ankle. That he was especially healthy, fit, and, relatively speaking, still young would contribute to rapid and complete recovery, Borsoi had been told. And no recovery could be rapid enough. It was critical that he return fully to duty.

It was not so much that the injuries to his legs should not be known, but rather that they should not be seen to inhibit his abilities to lead the FLNA units now in this time of crisis. And leadership was more vital than ever now, as were the Leopards and the street gang people like them all across the United States. The burden of carrying on the war would fall exclusively on their shoulders until the massive reorganization required could be accomplished. It would take weeks at least, perhaps months.

Exactly two weeks had elapsed since Humphrey Hodges had—reluctantly—announced to him the destruction of the FLNA operation on Cedar Ridge Islands.

And by now, of course, the Federal Bureau of Investigation, the Marshal Service, the Central Intelligence Agency, Army Intelligence, the Royal Canadian Mounted Police, the Mexican Federal Police, and some of the larger and more efficient North American state and local law enforcement agencies would have the results of Charlie Lang's initial interrogations. They would already be placing under surveillance and eventually arresting everyone on a list that would grow longer each time Lang was spoken with. The man's memory was phenomenal, unfortunately. Already Borsoi was aware of more than two hundred arrests. Very likely there had been more.

And he—Borsoi—was considered dead. That oversight would be rectified shortly.

"They're comin', Mr. Johnson." Reefer, his driver and his almost constant companion since his injuries, spoke from beside him. Borsoi felt himself starting to look on Reefer with a certain rough affection. There was ability there, to a degree, and far greater loyalty. "See 'em?" Reefer started to open his door.

"Yes, Reefer—I see them. Stay behind the wheel. There is no reason for you to get out."

Leopards leader Smitty stopped six feet or so from the

passenger side where Borsoi sat, saying "You're lookin' better, Mr. Johnson."

"I'm feeling better." With the Leopard leader Borsoi recognized six of the gang leader's most trusted lieutenants. He studied their faces, saying nothing, waiting for the tall, well-muscled young man to speak.

The leader of the Leopards and now, since Borsoi's coming, the leader of three more of the most powerful street gangs in Metro, cleared his throat. "I got your guys. A big-shot computer genius with the army who got himself a nose problem." He grinned a little as he snorted, to emphasize the—to him—humor implicit in a supposedly straight person being hooked on cocaine. "He can handle the stuff you need done when we're in. And I got the guys to get him in."

Then he looked at his six lieutenants, giving them a nod. They walked off. He looked at Reefer, nodding toward the other end of the alley. As Reefer started to climb out of the car, Borsoi placed a restraining hand on his right forearm.

The Leopard leader shrugged, then continued. "None of 'em knows they ain't comin' back. The car's rigged so if they make it out alive, they get blown to shit anyway. Arnie's getting real good with that explosives stuff. You made a good pick teachin' him."

"Thank you."

The Leopard leader laughed a little. "Didn't know the bomb he made was to blow himself up. Ha! So? What's next? Why the missile thing?"

Borsoi smiled benevolently. "It is called a missile battery. And, if your cocaine-addicted computer wizard is all he's cracked up to be—" Leopard leader didn't catch the pun. Borsoi went on anyway. "If he's as good as you say and sets in those coordinates I've provided perfectly, tomorrow morning's newspapers and television programs will have something very interesting to be shocked about. And the government of the United States will know the FLNA isn't out of business," Borsoi concluded with a smile.

CHAPTER

9

Tommy Chasen's wife was staring at him oddly. "What's the matter?" He looked away from her and returned his gaze to the kitchen table. He wasn't hungry for the macaroni and cheese, wasn't hungry for anything in the apartment, including his wife.

"I'm worried about you, all right?"

He didn't look at her. He'd memorized her looks—pretty enough—two years ago when he'd married her because she was pregnant, and, after all that, it turned out she wasn't pregnant. He'd been the first guy she'd ever done it with and she'd been so scared, she'd had what they called a hysterical pregnancy. Swelled up like anything, even after she knew it wasn't real. By that time they were married.

He'd had to quit school to support her because in the army nobody got paid enough, and he gave up the college classes to get a part-time job. Between the army in the day and the credit card company at night, there wasn't much time for bed. And when there was, it was usually for sleeping.

Jeanette had felt guilty, he figured, for messing up his

life so badly, so she got a job once the swelling went away. And that helped for a while. He'd almost had it set so he could go back to school in the evenings when the thing with the FLNA got started. The convenience store Jeanette worked in was burned down when the synagogue at the other end of the block was firebombed. The firemen were already too busy fighting a bunch of other fires to keep the fire from spreading. It consumed the whole block, and when the gas pumps outside the convenience store went up, three firemen were killed and the firestorm engulfed another block and a half.

Jobs were getting harder and harder to come by, especially for people like Jeanette. She didn't have a high school diploma, and factories and the like were closing down because they couldn't get night-shift workers.

Everybody was extending their credit past the breaking point, so there was plenty of work for him when he got off duty. He could catch overtime by getting in to work by around six P.M. and working through until four instead of three.

And he needed every dime.

It was Danny Hilliard who'd introduced him to snorting cocaine. He would have killed Danny, but Danny was in one of the bars they all used to go to—the one where Tommy Chasen had first met Jeanette—when the place was firebombed by the FLNA. Revenge and his source of supply were blotted out at once.

The rush had kept him going. The rush now dominated him. He knew that, Jeanette knew that. Maybe it was true that a lot of people who were hooked on cocaine didn't know they were, but he knew it. He put down the razor blade. Drug rehabilitation might work, but when was there the time for it? He still needed money, more than the army paid him. Without the cocaine, perhaps he wouldn't need the money; but he'd needed the money before the cocaine. And if he got into drug rehabilitation, the provost marshal's office would start investigating him for sure to see how he'd financed the habit; they'd find out how.

After Danny Hilliard died, it had been awful. He'd been without the stuff and going crazy until he found Stan Porembski. Stan sold to a lot of people in the military, was military himself.

And, through Stan, he met the FLNA.

Stan had given him some free that first time. After that it was pay or dry up. He'd tried booze. That didn't help. Joints didn't help either. He went back to Porembski and got down on his knees and begged for it, even offered Jeanette. He'd sold his watch, sold the good car and drove a pile of junk, sold everything he could sell except Jeanette.

And the final irony of it was that Stan had laughed, didn't want Jeanette.

Tommy Chasen snorted the first line. Jeanette was crying. He could hear her.

He'd mellowed out, would have been relaxed, except for what he was doing. The punk named Arnie sat beside him. Stan drove. Three more punks like Arnie sat in the backseat of the Dodge. He'd been promised enough money that he could get away, start over again. If Jeanette didn't like it, she could stay behind. She was the cause of all of his problems to begin with. The money would keep him going, get him set up in a little computer business, as he'd been thinking about for a long time now, and would keep him supplied until he had enough money and the business was running well enough that he could go in for rehabilitation and kick the cocaine.

He wondered, almost absently, if once he had kicked the cocaine, he would feel badly about tonight.

He'd asked them why they were going to break into the base and Stan had said, "We want to show the government that even their military installations aren't safe from us. We're going to program that antitank battery so, when we launch, they've got missiles dropping in parking lots and vacant lots all over Metro. And when we do that, they'll listen, know we have them. Then we can negotiate."

Tommy Chasen didn't know if he really believed Stan, but what else could they have planned besides just random terror? And Stan had told him, hadn't he, that the FLNA had abandoned that policy a long time ago. It was the Patriots who were responsible for terror attacks nowadays, in order to gain public sympathy.

Chasen had always distrusted the right-wing lunatic fringe anyway, and why would Stan lie? What purpose would be served?

"Put in the plugs," Stan advised as he turned the Dodge into the drive leading toward the battery's front gate.

Chasen felt like Batman or something using nose plugs, but Stan insisted that they wear them lest some of the gas seep into the car. Chasen started to put them into his nostrils, which were perpetually irritated. The noseplugs only added to the irritation.

And with them in, he could hardly breathe.

There were the documents, and they might get them in. Everybody was dressed in fatigues, even Arnie and the other punks, with short haircuts. So long as only he—Tommy—and Stan opened their mouths, maybe it would be all right and they wouldn't have to use the gas.

Or the guns.

CHAPTER
10

Director Cerillia's voice was hushed as he spoke. "It's good that you're fit enough for this, Luther." It was hard to hear anything at all with the constant hum of background chatter. The director's whispers were barely audible.

"Thank you, sir. I'm fine." He wasn't really fine, but that was no one's concern but his own. If he moved his right leg the wrong way, he was in agony.

Cerillia nodded his head. They kept walking, Steel moving deliberately to minimize any noticeable limp. Bill Runningdeer, Tom LeFleur, Clark Pietrowski, and Randy Blumenthal surrounded them. Despite the nature of the conference, despite the fact that the only personnel allowed to be armed inside the conference site were Federal Bureau of Investigation, Marshal Service, and Secret Service (not even federal judges were allowed to carry guns past the electronic security station on the first floor), Luther Steel had decreed his men be in readiness.

Steel caught a fleeting glimpse of the President for an instant, conferring with the Vice President, then a wall of Secret Service personnel obscured both men from view.

Bill Runningdeer, minus his Uzi, ran interference, as Cerillia led them toward one of the small conference rooms off the main assembly area. The director began to speak again, and Steel strained to hear. "We have heavy problems, Luther. Very heavy. Speaker Makowski is making waves, claims he has evidence of collusion between the President and David Holden. He's just politically ambitious enough to put the interests of himself and his party over the interests of the nation and blow everything wide open. The House Committee on Domestic Violence is planning on issuing subpoenas. Rumor has it that the President and I are both on the list. Roman Makowski'd crucify the President if he got the chance—literally. All from this Metro thing."

"I'm sorry, Mr. Director. It seemed like the best thing to—"

Cerillia clapped Steel on the shoulder as Runningdeer held open the door for them and they entered the conference room. "Nothing to be sorry for, Luther. Because of your efforts and the efforts of the Patriots, Metro had a free election, even if the winner was a socialist wimp and got himself assassinated afterward. There was a big carryover effect. Got out the vote in cities all around the nation. Elected some FLNA-ers, I'm sure, but probably put some good people into office too. You may have the same deal again with the special election in Metro slated for two months from now. We'll see if any of us are still on the streets by then."

The sparsely decorated room was well lit. Runningdeer checked through the Venetian blinds as Director Cerillia seated himself at the small desk at the far end by the windows. LeFleur and Blumenthal were by the door as Clark Pietrowski checked under pictures and inside lamps for bugs. This was all reminiscent of some third-rate political spy story, and Luther Steel was sickened by the whole thing.

Mr. Cerillia waved him into a chair and he took it, his right thigh hurting a little. It was almost healed, but the glass had cut deeply and, worse than the occasional spasm of pain, like that which he experienced now, was the itching. It was almost incessant. The doctor said it was a good sign of healing.

The FBI director spoke again. "Roman Makowski and his people are convinced that the back of the FLNA has been broken and now that it's just a cleanup operation, the time is ripe to blame the President for everything that happened. He controls that House Committee on Domestic Violence like a puppeteer. They're recommending a permanent ban on civilian ownership of handguns plus a bounty system. They're also recommending a federally funded jobs program—nothing to help the businesses this thing has crippled, though. And they're recommending amnesty for FLNA personnel not directly associated with a homicide."

"They're *what?*"

"They want to put everybody the Justice Department and the state and local people are nailing right back on the street. It's part of the Penal Reform Act—that's what they call it. It'll all be hitting the news by tomorrow morning. And there's a possibility Makowski will have that subpoena list unofficially leaked to some of his friends in the media. It will blunt everything the President will be able to do here. Ask you a question, Luther?"

Steel licked his lips. "Yes, sir?"

"Do you think we've crushed the FLNA or just given them a major setback? Honest answer. That's what I expect from you."

Steel cleared his throat. "Sir, ahh—no. We haven't done anything to permanently stop them. Sure, all that stuff Lang keeps feeding us—only half of which is verifiable or current—is helping us make some important arrests. And the loss of Cedar Ridge Islands had to have adversely affected them. But I'd estimate that we set them back by no more than six months, probably less. Some of the names Charlie Lang has been giving us are big people, rich people, well-connected people. We can't even get a warrant for some of them when all it's based on is the word of a convicted felon turned traitor. I think the FLNA is pulling back a little—and that worries me because it must mean they have something really big planned. We hurt them, but they aren't throwing in the towel. They're laughing at us right now because people like Speaker Makowski are saying the crisis has passed. He's playing right into their hands."

Mr. Cerillia leaned back in his chair, making a tent of his fingers across his vested chest. "Do you think Makowski is one of them, or just self-serving and politically ambitious?"

"I have no evidence on which I could postulate such a decision, sir. I would have to assume—" Steel cleared his throat.

"Assume what, Luther?"

"That he's just a run-of-the-mill ass, sir."

Mr. Cerillia began to laugh. Luther Steel felt uncomfortable. His wife would not have liked him making a remark like that. It was inviting trouble.

"I agree," Director Cerillia said after a moment. "But he's a dangerous ass. He's the same man who urged passage of a resolution that would have authorized Congress to independently negotiate with the FLNA. All he wants is publicity because he translates that into votes for himself and his party and a chance of defeating the President. He's about as vile as they come. Nothing is more important to him than his own ambition."

Luther Steel didn't quite know what to say.

Director Cerillia continued speaking. "What I want you to understand, Luther, is that if Roman Makowski subpoenas the President and the President reveals the situation that has unofficially existed so successfully between the Bureau and the Patriots, your tail may be in the wringer."

Luther Steel shifted uncomfortably in his seat, telling himself it was the wound to his right thigh.

"You wouldn't go down alone, obviously. The President will assume full responsibility, and I'll assume equal responsibility. But if Makowski's in a mood for blood, you'll be bleeding right along with us. Your men should be all right. I just wanted you to understand that whatever transpires, you've earned the undying gratitude of both the President and myself and you've performed a service of immeasurable value to your nation. We'll be behind you all the way, but that may not help. I'm saying this so you can consider your options, Luther."

Luther Steel thought about his wife, about the children. He cleared his throat. "I'm not quitting until they take my badge away, sir. And maybe not after that."

Cerillia smiled. "I expected no less." And he looked at his watch. "We'd better move." He stood up; Steel stood as well. Cerillia extended his hand. "You're a good man; but of course, I knew that when I tapped you for this assignment. Remember that good men often fall prey to lesser men. It's the only way lesser men can justify their own existence at times."

"Yes, sir."

Cerillia began walking across the room, LeFleur with

his hand on the doorknob, Clark Pietrowski exiting, Runningdeer behind him.

The group passed through the doorway as the President of the United States ascended the podium.

CHAPTER

11

Tommy Chasen's palms were sweating. He wiped them down the sides of his fatigue pants. Getting onto base since the FLNA attacks had begun was no longer the simple thing it once was. A pass system had been initiated. A new pass with a color code and number code that could be read by laser scanner was issued each time a person left the base and was handed in when the person returned to the base.

Stan Porembski rolled down his window. He addressed the sentry by name. "Hey, Bill—how's it goin'?"

"Stan—let's see your passes, huh?"

Porembski handed over his while Chasen glanced at Arnie and the other three street punks. They were pulling passes out of breast pockets of their fatigue blouses. Their passes were fake, of course. The genuine articles were controlled under tight security by the provost marshal's office. Only Porembski's and his own pass were legitimate.

Chasen handed over his pass. Would the laser scanner run over just one or two of the passes, or all of them? He shivered involuntarily as he considered the possibilities.

Gambling on getting into the base by sheer luck seemed stupid, unprofessional. He'd asked Porembski why there wasn't a better system. Stan had replied that he shouldn't worry and left it at that.

The guard—Bill—took the passes, looking into the car as he did. "I never seen you guys before," he said, directing his eyes first toward Arnie, then the three in the backseat.

Stan Porembski reached out toward the man.

Chasen saw it as if it were in slow motion. He started to shout. The thing in Porembski's hand looked like some kind of gun, but it wasn't the right shape.

A gray-white cloud appeared near its muzzle, partially enveloping the guard's face. The guard's eyes suddenly went wide, his body rocking back.

"Stan!" Tommy exclaimed.

"Shut up," Porembski told him, holding a handkerchief over his mouth and powering up the window.

In a second all three of the street punks from the backseat were out of the car, handkerchiefs over their mouths. As Tommy Chasen started to speak, he felt a prodding against his ribcage.

This was clearly a gun. And Arnie had it leveled at him.

The President cleared his throat and went on. "With the recent success of the United States Justice Department against the Cedar Ridge Islands base used by the Front for the Liberation of North America as a staging area for infiltration of overseas nationals, some may think that the war is won. Nothing, ladies and gentlemen, could be further from the truth. A major battle has been won, yes, and thanks to the courageous men of the FBI and other Justice Department personnel, an important victory. But only that—not the war, not yet.

"Intelligence reports indicate," he continued, "that the FLNA is heavily financed and sponsored by certain elements within the Third World and also within the Soviet bloc." There were muted murmurs from the audience as the President paused. He smiled almost benignly then. "But there is no evidence to indicate that the FLNA is the official policy arm of any nation, including the obvious choice." There was subdued laughter. "It appears that certain unidentified radical elements acting unofficially within the hierarchy of the Soviet bloc in conjunction with certain Third World governments noted for their anti-American sentiments and their use of violence as an instrument of national policy have coalesced for the express purpose of destroying our nation and the nations of Mexico and Canada from within. So far we haven't stopped them. And we're not about to stop them by lulling ourselves into complacency, thinking we've already won a war the enemy is still fighting and fully intends to win. And, ladies and gentlemen, this is a war—make no mistake!"

It was somewhat of a thrill, actually, to be sitting in the same auditorium where the President of the United States was speaking. There was a certain electricity in the air from all the security surrounding the Vice President, the Secretary of State, and various officials from Mexico and the Canadian government.

It was a thrill akin to the first time he'd seen the Queen and, wholly by accident, been introduced to her.

Chief Inspector Morrison, at his elbow, whispered, "I doubt a mosquito could get in here, with all the Secret Service and FBI personnel and all."

He nodded, smiling to himself. Of course, he had gotten through several identity checks and no one was the wiser that he wasn't with the Royal Canadian Mounted Police at all. Yet the forgeries were official ones, designed to be scrutiny-proof, and he was in the company of one of Canada's most well-known police officials.

He supposed his nervousness was the result of being unarmed in a place where virtually everyone else was armed, and armed heavily.

The President declared, "We will not surrender to the forces of anarchy, nor will we surrender to something which is equally destructive, the degeneracy of apathy!" There was a standing ovation beginning and, at once not to call attention to himself and because he genuinely approved the President's sentiments, Geoffrey Kearney stood as well and applauded vigorously.

Kearney's eyes shifted about the auditorium. How vulnerable was the conference, really? They were on the sixteenth floor of an office building that had been cleared of all personnel except those directly involved as participants in the conference or as security for it. On the roof above them, three helicopters and one Harrier jet fighter —he'd flown a Harrier and liked them—were poised and waiting to whisk away any of the notables at the first sign of trouble. More Harrier jets were in readiness in the parking lot to provide air security for the President, the highest-ranking official present. The area within one square mile was considered secure. Jet fighter aircraft flew patterns over the area centering on the office building, which was owned by the telephone company. Its use had been donated for the conference. The building was officially still under construction, cranes and other building machines in evidence, some of the lower floors not wholly walled in.

Yet Kearney wondered.

It was the sort of situation where a firearm would likely do little good, yet he still felt slightly naked without one. Still, if things went badly, he could likely catch up a weapon; there were certainly enough around him to choose from. The Secret Service openly, yet tastefully, were carrying Uzis. Uzis were a fine weapon, of course, but required considerable training to counteract their speed, which tended to make full magazines empty in a matter of seconds, leaving the untrained or improperly trained user with an expensive bludgeon.

Geoffrey Kearney mentally shrugged as he sat down and returned his attention to the President, who was continuing. "The time for decision is upon us, ladies and gentlemen. Do we fight the good fight and preserve democracy, or do we cower and await our doom? I say we fight!" Another standing ovation, Kearney and Morrison, beside him, were standing, applauding.

Kearney whispered to Morrison, "That black fellow standing beside Rudolph Cerillia—that's Luther Steel, isn't it?"

"Yes—I think so."

"Good—I'd fancy an introduction to him."

"I'll arrange it, of course."

"Good."

The President began to speak again. . . .

The sentries were dead. Tommy Chasen had to remind himself of that, that this was all real. And that Stan Porembski had lied to him.

If he'd lied about that—

The car stopped, the eighteen-wheeler that had so suddenly appeared at the gate the moment the guards were killed angling up beside them. The garage where the

ATGMs, mounted on their half-tracks, were parked was just ahead of them.

"Out," Porembski said.

"Wait a minute."

Porembski looked at him. "What is it, Tommy?"

"Just what's the truck for? And what kind of program am I putting into the guidance computer anyway?"

Porembski shrugged his shoulders as he climbed out from behind the wheel followed by Arnie. He lit a cigarette with a disposable lighter. "One of the ATGM launchers is getting loaded aboard the truck for another mission. You're feeding a new set of coordinates into the other one while Arnie changes the warheads from training to high explosive. Ever drive past that new telephone company building?"

"The one—"

"The one with the upper floors all finished and that nice big flat roof. That's the one, Tommy. Well, those coordinates you're going to feed into the multiple-launch guided missile system for that tank killer array are going to launch those missiles right at that building. The laser targeting eye will be in place in—" Porembski checked his watch. "In about six minutes. It should take a nose-hungry pro like you about four minutes to lay in the new coordinates. Arnie's new warheads will be in position sometime in the middle there. All twelve 230mm rockets will launch in ripple-fire sequence. That building'll be just a memory."

"Why, Stan?" Chasen was feeling sick.

"Because if you don't, I'll kill you. And I'll kill your little wife just for good measure. But before I kill you, I'll chain you up to a wall and let you stare at enough cocaine to put you in heaven, and all the time you'll be just enough outa reach of it so that you'll be in hell. And after you've gone all the way around and back and I'm tired of watching you beg and try rippin' your skin off just to get free and snort it, then I'll kill you. That's why? I got any problems with you, Tommy, huh?"

Tommy Chasen looked down at his hands and sniffed. "No. No." He sniffed again. "No problems."

"Good."

Chasen got out of the car. He wanted to do something heroic, something to stop this. But he was past that, he knew. And he wouldn't ask any more questions, like who was in the building he'd be wiping off the face of the earth, or anything like that. He felt as if he hated himself, or should, because he wanted to ask Stan if they were still going to give him the money and the cocaine and keep their promise.

But he was afraid to ask that, to ask anything more.

Maybe the MPs would come, stop it all.

He heard the ripping and tearing sound as the metal of the doors to the garage surrendered under the cutters. The doors were thrown open.

Lights went on and he followed Porembski inside to see two half-track–mounted, laser-aimed, free-flight anti-tank guided missile arrays.

His mind tripped into technical. A designator, airborne perhaps, or at some ground location with a clear line of sight on the building, would place the laser beam on the target. He was no missile expert, but his familiarity with computers gave him a basic knowledge of guidance and weapons systems. At the back of his mind he remembered something about such a unit as this being able to drop all its missiles into an area the size of a football field. The telephone building that was being erected was more than that size.

It would be like shooting fish in a barrel. He backed

away as the nearer of the two units began to rumble forward on wheels and treads, heading for the garage door. Range was somewhere in the neighborhood of twenty thousand meters. He tried figuring the distance to the target. It was substantially less than six miles away, easily accessible.

The second half-track rumbled to life, inching forward as if the driver were having trouble controlling it, then moving smoothly enough into the first vehicle's wake. Tommy Chasen looked through the doors. The first unit was stopping, the stabilizing jacks lowering for deployment. The rear of the eighteen-wheeler was opening. It was the shape of a moving van, only larger, higher, slightly wider than an ordinary semi.

A ramp was let down, the second vehicle moving toward it. If this were planned for the twelve rockets in the first battery, what was planned for the second vehicle? he wondered.

"Get to work." Porembski smiled and then rubbed his finger along the side of his nose like St. Nicholas in the Christmas poem. "We've got something for you when you're through, man."

Chasen took the handwritten set of coordinates, looked at them. It would take no effort and little time before the reprogramming would be complete.

And what Porembski had for him he needed more than he had needed anything ever in his life.

CHAPTER

12

Clark Pietrowski suddenly crouched beside him, his voice a hoarse whisper. "Boss, we got problems."

Luther Steel turned in his seat, looked into Pietrowski's eyes, then at Rudolph Cerillia. "Sir—"

"Keep me informed." The director nodded.

Steel was up, moving, grateful for the opportunity to exercise his stiffening right leg.

Chief Inspector Lionel Morrison of the Royal Canadian Mounted Police was speaking, detailing the successes and failures of a joint FBI/RCMP task force assembled to stem the flow of FLNA personnel back and forth across the U.S./Canadian border. Morrison was an interesting speaker, Steel thought.

As Steel followed Pietrowski along the aisle toward the rear of the auditorium, a man rose from the end seat. He was tall and lean, but obviously fit under the well-tailored charcoal-gray suit. His black knit tie swung free like a pendulum beneath the firm jawline as he moved his left hand at his necktie while his right buttoned a single button of the suit's jacket. "I say—you're Special Agent Steel, aren't you? I'm Kearney, with the RCMP. Chief

Inspector Morrison promised to introduce us. Anything up?" He extended his right hand. The grip was dry and firm.

The voice was a low, well-modulated whisper, the accent more like something out of a British movie than any Canadian Steel had ever met. Steel had a choice: stand in the aisle and explain (lie) or let the fellow come along. "I'm Steel—good to meet you. Maybe you can help."

Steel walked on. Kearney fell in step beside him, murmuring behind his hand, "I hear the chief inspector all the time—and anyway, he rehearsed the speech on me during the flight down to Metro." The man—Kearney, was it?—was surveying the room, as if looking for something. Steel made a mental bet that Kearney had some background in executive protection.

They reached the end of the aisle, Runningdeer and LeFleur joining them, Runningdeer saying, "Randy's looking for a mirror."

"What the hell's Blumenthal doing looking for a mirror?"

Kearney butted in. "Sounds to me like someone's spotted a laser targeting system on the building, right?" He smiled, his eyes—which were dark—positively twinkling, his cheeks seaming with it, almost like elongated dimples. He ran the fingers of his left hand back through the full shock of wavy brown hair, hair tumbling back over his forehead at the side just as it had been before the obviously futile gesture.

"The Brit's got it." Pietrowski nodded gravely as they moved through the auditorium doors and into the lobby.

"Who's in charge of ordering an evacuation?" Kearney asked easily.

Steel looked at him. "The director." Then he looked at Clark Pietrowski. "A laser?"

"Could be for targeting. My age, you're not too much into lasers, unless it's in some outer space movie or somethin'."

"It's a laser," Runningdeer said.

"I was smoking a cigarette and I had a window open to look out," LeFleur said. "The smoke all of a sudden turned red."

"That mirror won't work to deflect the laser, by the way. The laser will burn right through it most likely," Kearney said.

"Who the hell is he?" Runningdeer interjected.

Kearney extended his right hand. "Geoffrey Kearney, RCMP. Bit of a counterterrorism expert, actually. Are we evacuating, Agent Steel?"

Steel nodded, licked his lips, realizing that Kearney was pressuring him. "You sure of what you saw, Tom?" Steel asked LeFleur.

"Sure."

"Get Randy; scrap the mirror idea. Mr. Kearney's right. Bill, you go with Randy. Get security rolling up on the roof." He looked at Pietrowski. "Clark—tell Mr. Cerillia it's my opinion the building is under attack and should be evacuated at once."

"Right, boss."

Steel took the small radio from his belt. "This is Steel to command central. You're about to get a coitus interruptus from Director Cerillia. Let's get everybody into the right slot. Out."

Kearney was looking at him, smiling oddly. "Coitus interruptus?"

"Pull-out." Steel nodded.

"That's marvelous—really marvelous! What can I do to help?"

Steel weighed the possibilities, then decided. "Pray."

Kearney cleared his throat. "Capital idea, under the circumstances."

The Secret Service were already moving the President and the Vice President toward the elevators cordoned off for their use. Chief Inspector Morrison stopped speaking and Director Cerillia rose. "Excuse me, Chief Inspector Morrison, ladies and gentlemen," he began, stepping into the aisle. "I have been given word that the building may be under attack. We need to evacuate immediately following the procedures outlined in the emergency action briefing we all attended this morning."

All of a sudden everyone started from the chairs.

Steel looked at LeFleur. "Get in there fast. Stay with Mr. Cerillia. Don't let him out of your sight. Make sure he's on one of those choppers. Whatever it takes, right?"

"Gotchya, Luther." LeFleur was gone, shouldering his way along the aisle.

Steel looked at Kearney. "Anything I can do to help, Agent Steel? My chief inspector should be long gone for the roof by now."

Steel looked toward the nearest set of emergency doors. "The roof. Let's go."

Steel ran toward the doors. As he punched them open, an alarm sounded, but in the next instant another alarm started to sound. A prerecorded message was blaring over the speaker system. "The building is under aerial attack. Proceed to your designated evacuation site in an orderly manner. Personnel are waiting to assist you. There is no cause for alarm."

Steel looked behind him. Kearney was laughing.

CHAPTER

13

Chasen looked up from the computer console. "It's done."

"Good." Porembski looked pleased.

The eighteen-wheeler was already moving. There had been no armed response from the base yet. But their entry had been slick, noiseless. Two men who'd dropped off from the cab of the eighteen-wheeler had taken up the guard positions. Maybe the guards' deaths and the penetration of the base hadn't been discovered—yet. There would be hell to pay when it was.

Porembski quickened his pace. "Sixty seconds until firing," he said, glancing at his watch. "Then the whole face of this fascist pig country will change, everything will be turned around." And he looked over his shoulder at Chasen, telling him, "You helped to change history, bring history in line with reality, fulfill the destiny of mankind."

Chasen merely nodded, as if he understood or cared. He was in pain and he really couldn't think. "Yes. That stuff you have for me—shit, I can really use it. My nerves are fried."

"Only thirty seconds now." Porembski stopped beside the car, looking back toward the rocket launcher. "History."

"I could really use the stuff—I'm hurting."

Porembski smiled at him as they neared the car. "You'll never have to worry about pain again, my man. Never have to worry about it again."

There was a gun in Stan Porembski's hand and Chasen started to speak, to tell him that he didn't understand, but then there was a rumbling from behind him—*boom, boom, boom, boom,* over and over again. A wind tore at him, and Porembski raised his eyes toward the missiles streaking overhead away from the launcher. Chasen started to run, made one step, felt a sudden emptiness in the pit of his stomach, then again in his chest, and the emptiness there was replaced with fire as he fell back, tails of fire streaking across the sky overhead.

On the wide, flat roof of the new still under-construction building, the camouflage-painted Harrier vertical takeoff and landing jet fighter carrying the President of the United States was becoming airborne. Other Harriers rose like wasps from the parking lot below; helicopters circled the upper stories of the building.

Luther Steel started to turn away, looking for Director Cerillia, to get him to safety; but Kearney, the RCMP man, grabbed at Steel's arm. "Look, there!"

Streaks of fire were etching inward off the horizon, moving so quickly they were hard for the eye to follow as more than a blur.

Steel reached for his radio as he started to run. The Vice President was fewer than ten yards from him, boarding a Bell helicopter. In the instant that he spoke, Steel realized that the Vice President would be killed and so would he. "This is Steel—missile attack. Get the President off faster! Missile—"

There was a rushing sound like a high wind and a blinding flash of light, then another and another and Luther Steel was falling, reaching to hold on, the radio gone from his fingers, nothing to hold onto, flames. . . .

Beside him, when he opened his eyes, there was a human hand, partially blackened. No body was nearby that it was connected to. Simply the hand.

Luther Steel recognized the hand from the Annapolis ring on one of the fingers and the missing tip of the little finger. The Vice President of the United States had served as a naval fighter pilot until a freak accident robbed him of a digit. Then he'd retired, entered politics, and served two terms in the House, one in the Senate, before being tapped, rather unexpectedly, as number-two man on his party's ticket.

Luther Steel closed his eyes, the weight of the beam across his chest too much to bear.

CHAPTER

14

Secret Service agents—they were as easy to spot as a piece of shit in a Caesar salad, Roman Makowski had always thought—were coming into the restaurant through the front entrance and through the doors leading from the kitchen. Two had the effrontery to display their machine guns or whatever they were in the open, in public.

And then Makowski saw a young man he recognized, a clerk at the Supreme Court. The clerk broke away from the knot of Secret Service who now had the entire dining room encircled. He strode toward the table Roman Makowski shared with Horace Elderton and Elderton's very pretty and very smart legislative aide, Nancy O'Donnell.

Makowski stood, dropping his napkin to his chair.

"Mr. Speaker," the young clerk began, then cleared his throat. "Or should I say 'Mr. President'—"

Makowski looked at his luncheon companions in turn. Horace Elderton was chief lobbyist for People for a Better America. The PBA was embarking on a multimillion-dollar campaign to support the legislative package endorsed by the House Committee on Domestic Violence, a legislative package Roman Makowski had just been discussing, had authored, would fight for. Then Nancy O'Donnell. Her pansy-blue eyes looked up at him. With the back of her hand she swept away a lock of almost black hair that had fallen across her forehead. He even liked the freckles that lurked beneath the seemingly minimal makeup. You could never tell about makeup, though. The President rarely used it when he made a speech, but he always looked as if he did. The Vice President, inclined toward being pale, used it whenever he was on television, but never looked as if he did. And women like Nancy O'Donnell, the pretty kind, just seemed to be naturally better at it. He found himself wondering, for some strange reason, what else she might be good at.

He looked away from her, looked at the clerk. "What's going on? Has something happened?"

"Sir—ahh—"

"Out with it!"

"There was some sort of missile attack—"

"Missiles! Holy—"

"Not Soviet missiles, sir—but our missiles, they figure. They were fired at the conference—"

"The telephone building, yes?"

"The President is in a coma, not expected to come out of it. The Vice President—his—"

"His what?" Makowski insisted.

"They found a left hand and a portion of torso that are identifiable as the Vice President's."

Makowski asked, "How can they identify a piece of his torso, for—" And he looked at Nancy O'Donnell, ready to apologize for sickening her. But she was made of stronger stuff, he realized.

The clerk was still speaking. "You're the President, sir.

By the rules of succession. The President is incapacitated and the Vice President is dead. You're the President and I'm to take you into the corridor where Justice Kruger will be arriving at any moment to swear you in, sir. You're the President."

Roman Makowski saw it in her eyes, a look of pride, maybe a look of something else.

And he looked at Elderton. The PBA executive merely whispered, "Congratulations, Mr. President."

Mr. President . . .

He'd awakened with a soreness in his head like nothing he'd ever experienced. Luckily he did not move. As he looked down, Geoffrey Kearney realized he was stretched out across a structural beam, that he had fallen through the roof. Smoke was everywhere. He was soaked in water.

Gingerly he attempted to move.

His back ached, but not so badly that he thought it broken. He could wiggle his toes, right enough.

The water.

It was coming from below the girder. He looked down, his head swimming with pain, his vision blurring so that he had to squint to regain some true perception.

He was in no imminent danger, he reckoned, unless he fell from the beam. Nothing was below him for several floors. He moved his hands to his neck, quickly undoing the knot of his black silk knit tie. He tugged the tie from around his neck. The end of the wider, forward-facing portion concealed a small pocket. From the pocket of his trousers he got his solid brass Zippo cigarette lighter. He inserted it into the pocket in the necktie, to weight the tie, then, leaning out slightly over the girder, he whipped the tie around beneath the girder and caught it with his other hand. After recovering his lighter and pocketing it, Kearney passed one end of the tie through his trouser belt, then tied a square knot, effectively safety-belting himself to the girder.

Then he leaned back, closing his eyes.

The Canadian government was undoubtedly correct in asking the help of his Service: "Send your best man, or at least the best one you don't mind so terribly much getting killed." Kearney imagined it had gone something like that. "We need someone to get into the U.S.A. and find the leader of this damned FLNA, find the fellow and eliminate him. When will your chap be round?"

He'd taken the first Concord out, been met by Lionel Morrison, barely had time to pose for the identity photos and shower and change, then boarded a Canadian military transport and flown to Metro as an RCMP counterterrorism specialist.

Whoever the FLNA leader was, it couldn't have been the fellow Borsoi. Borsoi was dead, of course, and someone had carefully planned this whole affair. Perhaps the American President had gotten off safely, perhaps not. The Vice President was certainly dead. The first missile had impacted almost directly on his helicopter. Would the Americans have another of their media free-for-all elections?

Or what if Borsoi wasn't dead?

It didn't really matter, Geoffrey Kearney thought as the pain in his head subsided a bit. Other pains in muscles he hadn't even recalled having started to surface as he came fully around.

Now it was personal, which was the best reason to kill without feeling remorse afterward.

Helicopters were flying about overhead, and he opened

his eyes. A loud hailer sounded. "You on the girder! Yo! Can you move?"

He couldn't possibly have shouted over the whirring of the rotor blades so he sat up, careful to keep his balance as he did so. It was already late afternoon from the look of the horizon. He wondered how long he'd been out. He checked the Rolex on his left wrist. The crystal was smashed.

He shrugged.

"Can you move?"

Kearney waved back, his right shoulder aching as he moved his arm.

"We're dropping a man onto the girder. You'll be all right. Take it easy and relax."

Kearney waved again, signaling that he understood. He didn't exactly envy the fellow who'd be dropping onto the girder, nor the pilot of the helicopter for that matter. He decided to wait it out, though, as he had no real assessment of his own injuries and how awkward they might make it for him to function.

Kearney leaned back, looking upward. He gauged that he'd fallen at least three floors. Then he gazed downward. There was nothing immediately below him for another several floors at least. If it hadn't been for the lucky inter-position of the girder on which he lay, he would have been dead.

Was it an act of providence or a bad joke of fate?

There was no way to tell.

"Hey—we're comin' in!"

He sat up again, watching the helicopter as it edged toward the building. Through the bubble, Kearney could see the worried look on the Howdy Doody–faced pilot. There was a man in the portside doorway of the helicop-ter. It was one of those bulky rescue types used by so many coast guards and navies around the world. The man, fitted with a white pack with a red cross emblazoned on it, was hitched to a rescue harness, the harness locked to a substantial-looking safety line and feeding out to a winch that was protruding some three feet or so from the side of the fuselage.

The intent was clear. Swing out to the winch, winch down to the girder, perform a cursory medical examination to ascertain whether the party could be moved without seriously exacerbating any injuries. Then into a chest harness or Swiss seat and get winched up to the chopper where hands would draw the injured person inside, and the winch would be lowered again for the rescue worker on the girder.

Kearney turned most of his mind to other matters. There would be interminable debriefings after the interminable physical examinations. Then a flight back to Toronto, hopefully with Morrison if he were still alive and able but with him or without him, then pick up the packet of things shipped out for him: American driver's licenses, credit cards, concealed carry permits for those areas where such documents were still valid in the United States, money, a few items of personal equipment, then back across the border to settle the score.

"Hey—fella! You all right?"

He opened his eyes, realizing he'd drifted off. Possibly it was the effect of the head injury. "Right as rain." Kearney smiled, starting to undo the square knot in his tie before the fellow cut it and ruined it.

CHAPTER

15

". . . and at this hour it is still uncertain as to the number of casualties." The pretty black woman's usually smiling face was grave as she read the news. "Unofficial Washington sources report—but it is at this moment impossible to confirm—that Speaker of the House Roman Makowski has been sworn in as what is termed 'acting President.' What exactly that implies as to the fate of both the President and the Vice President is unclear. We switch now to our chief Washington correspondent Richard Blumberg."

"This is Richard Blumberg reporting from the White House." He consulted what looked like a note card in his left hand. "At twelve thirty-four today, Secret Service personnel escorted House Speaker Roman Makowski to the White House lawn where the speaker boarded a special Harrier vertical takeoff jet and was flown to an undisclosed location, possibly the specially modified E-4 Boeing 747 that is the presidential airborne command post known as the *Doomsday Plane.* It is known that Speaker Makowski, a harsh critic of the current administration, especially of the administration's handling of the ongoing

struggle against the Front for the Liberation of North
America, contacted his office and advised legislative aides
to work toward postponing the rumored subpoenaing of
the President, and I quote, 'out of respect concerning
what has happened', unquote. White House spokesman
Harden Lassiter will be issuing a formal statement in just
about another ten minutes. Perhaps then we will know
how this strange turn of events is connected to the missile
attack this morning in Metro. Back to you, Irene."

"Thanks, Richard. We'll be rejoining Richard
Blumberg shortly for live coverage of that promised an-
nouncement by White House spokesman Harden
Lassiter. Meanwhile—" The picture shifted from her face
to tape of the site of the security conference taken only
moments after the missile attack. "These scenes, shot earlier today, show the extent of the damage to the upper
floors of the structure. One source, who refused to be
identified, labeled it 'a minor miracle' that the entire
building wasn't brought down. We have just gained access to a videotape shot by an onlooker at the time of the
actual attack. It is in VHS format and shot on a home
camera." The tape changed to a shaky picture, at an unnatural angle. The narration continued. "If you look in
the upper left corner of your screen, you can see the missile contrails as they home in on the target. There! There
again! One right after the other, impacting the roof of the
telephone company office building used as the site for the
top-secret international security conference. Harrier jet
fighter aircraft, like those in camouflage visible now at
the center of the screen, were to be used to carry away
the President and some of the other dignitaries in the
event of just such a disaster. Those are army helicopter
gunships crossing the screen now. Already fires are visible throughout the upper portion of the structure, and

those large chunks of debris falling to the right of your screen appear to be actual segments of the roof and upper floors—"

David Holden looked away from the television set. Rosie Shepherd held his hand.

Some of the Patriots around them wept, some whispered unintelligibly, others just stared at the screen.

CHAPTER
16

Luther Steel hung up the telephone. His wife had cried when she'd heard his voice, dropped the phone, told the children, "Daddy's all right!" and then cried some more when he'd told her he was in the hospital for observation.

She had asked, "How's the President, Luther?"

He'd told her that he didn't know and couldn't talk about it if he did, then said he'd call back and that he loved her. Then he hung up.

He didn't know, but he suspected. The President had to be dead.

He could still close his eyes and see the heat flash as the first missile struck. And, even with his eyes open, he would always see the hand of the Vice President there beside him on the floor. It had been three hours before rescue workers had removed the beam that had fallen across him, pinned him to the floor.

He had told them about the hand, but the man who seemed to be in charge said, "I don't know anything about it." When Steel had looked again, the hand was gone. The drugs they had given him made him too weak to move, too tired to think straight for very long, and breathing was difficult. The doctors had told him that there was no internal damage immediately apparent, that he had several fractured ribs and a sprained ankle, and that he was very lucky.

Miraculously, all the members of his team were still alive, all injured but none gravely.

The door opened.

"Luther."

It was Director Cerillia, a patch bandage by his left temple, right arm in a sling. Two men, obviously FBI but their faces unfamiliar, flanked him.

"Wait outside," the director ordered, closing the door. "Luther, the President is in a coma. It's doubted he'll live. The Vice President is dead. Roman Makowski was sworn in several hours ago as acting President, if that's the right term. Do you need me to call your wife?"

"I did it, sir."

"Good. The rest of your men—Pietrowski, Blumenthal, Runningdeer, and LeFleur—I understand they're all going to be all right."

"Yes, sir."

"This isn't like a new administration coming in, everybody in a position like mine who's been appointed turning in a perfunctory resignation. The news is leaking out. There's going to be a news conference in about another two minutes. Harden Lassiter is breaking some of the details to the press. The newspaper people haven't gotten around to you yet. When they do, don't say anything you don't want splashed all over the headlines. Makowski will use this as a means of taking me down—this attack —because we were partially responsible for security. He'll try to take you and everyone else closely associated with me. But we can't let that happen. I won't resign until the President dies. That could be hours or weeks or months. The doctors don't know. There's a slim chance he might survive, but there's a better than even bet that if he did he'd be permanently brain damaged and unable to resume leadership. What I'm saying," Director Cerillia said, "is that once I'm gone, this country's still going to need men like you. Just don't do anything stupid like quitting or putting yourself into the hot seat."

"How many dead, sir?"

"Nobody knows. Most of the Canadian delegation is still unaccounted for, except for Lionel Morrison and the fellow who walked out with you, Kearney I think his name was. I don't remember. The chief of the Mexican delegation is in guarded condition officially. Unofficially he isn't expected to last the night. We tracked the origin of the missiles—the army base seven miles from the site of the conference. An unknown number of persons, presumably with real I.D., broke in and killed then replaced the sentries, utilized one of the antitank guided missile launchers stored there for the attack, stole another one and got away with it. Somebody pretty talented had to be involved because there were practice warheads on the missiles and they had to be replaced. There are a few clues. A computer expert—army—was found dead at the scene, shot several times with a medium-caliber handgun. He's likely the one responsible for reprogramming the launch coordinates, the actual hands-on job. Preliminary tests showed cocaine in his system, so we may have some of the motivation behind his act. His wife's being interrogated by our people and the army now. And there's a man who was a known associate of the dead man, also army, who's missing. His name is Porembski. That's all we have. God knows what they'll do with that second launcher. Another twelve missiles they can launch all at once or separately."

"Is Speaker Makowski safe at least, sir?" Steel asked, not really caring for the man but holding the deepest respect for the office Makowski now—he prayed temporarily—filled.

"He's aboard the *Doomsday Plane*. The Soviets are complaining about that. I guess it's the safest place for him."

"I guess, sir."

"You get some rest. Your family okay?"

"They're fine, sir."

"If things go as I think, you'll be more important than ever to this, Luther. I know you won't fail me. Hang in there. Whatever they say, whatever lies they tell, hang tough."

"Yes, sir."

Director Cerillia only nodded, then opened the door, stepped out, and pulled the door closed behind him.

Luther Steel stared at the door until the drugs made him fall asleep again.

CHAPTER
17

Tom Ashbrooke stood on the balcony, overlooking the gently upsweeping wall of the valley below where the chalet perched. His eyes followed the green until it gave way to the white-splotched gray of the peaks only a few miles distant.

"Tom?" Diane's voice.

"I'm all right." He turned around and looked at her. She was beautiful, as she always was. Her hair had begun to gray when she was in her early thirties, been almost totally gray since she was in her middle forties. She had never dyed it. He had asked her once why she didn't. Her figure was as perfect as a woman of twenty-five, with or without her clothes on, the exercise she had always taken (not just to be faddish or to control her figure) evident in the firm chin, firm arms, beautifully firm breasts. Without the gray hair, she would have looked half her fifty-four years, he'd always felt. She'd joked with him, saying she didn't want to look too young and make him appear more the cradle robber than he really was, then finally said she'd dye it if he wanted her to. She'd never dyed it. "You'll be cold out here." She wore a collarless white cotton sweater with long sleeves, a camel-color skirt that came almost to her ankles, flat shoes, her shoulders hunched slightly and her arms hugged around her over her chest. She tossed her head, her past shoulder-length hair like something that had a life of its own. He was glad she'd never dyed it. "I'm just trying to think."

She walked toward him, stood beside him. He put his arm around her shoulders and she leaned her head against his chest. "You wish you were there, don't you?"

"Who would have thought David and—gee."

"When Elizabeth and the children were—" She never seemed to say the word.

"Now a missile attack in Metro, the Vice President dead, the President comatose, that asshole Roman Makowski calling himself some kind of cockamamie acting President. Hell—"

"And?" She looked up into his eyes.

"And—"

"Maybe you should be back in the United States fighting bad guys instead of here in Switzerland living the quiet, good life?"

"Yeah, something like that. What do you think?"

"David's close to half your age, remember?"

Tom Ashbrooke shrugged. "I don't mean running around playing commando or anything, but—the Patriots. They sound like good Americans, Diane."

"They probably are. With Makowski as President, they won't have any chance at all. So—"

Tom Ashbrooke looked at his wife. "So?"

"How are you going to help them?"

"What?"

She leaned up on her toes and kissed him easily, comfortably on the lips. "I mean, well, ever since Elizabeth—" She looked away from him, shivered, her face turned toward the mountains. "Ever since she died— there. I said it. Ever since then, I've been wondering when. And since they started putting David's picture on the cover of all the news magazines, calling him some sort of right-wing vigilante. Well, I mean, Tom! How long have we been married?" Before he could answer, she said, "I just knew it was a matter of time, for God's sake. How will you contact him?"

"I don't know. It would've been nice if he'd tried contacting us, maybe." He lit a cigarette. He smoked rarely these days and, he supposed because of that, Diane had stopped complaining about it.

"But he didn't."

"I've got some friends who owe me some favors. Maybe, ahh—" He exhaled through his nostrils, the smoke dissipating quickly on the cool air.

"Just promise me one thing, Thomas."

She was serious, he knew, because she only used his full name when she was speaking in deadly earnest.

"What?"

"Don't ever get killed. We have our health. We have each other. That's important, Tom. It's more than so many people have. The money, this house, all of that isn't so important, really. What's important is us."

He felt her arms curl around his waist and he held her tighter to him. "Don't you think I know that?" Tom Ashbrooke whispered. After the loss of their daughter and their three grandchildren, if he went off and got himself killed it would kill her. "I won't get myself killed. You can take that to the bank, baby." He touched his lips to her hair.

CHAPTER
18

Humphrey Hodges sat in the chair beside the fireplace. The hearth was still. Dimitri Borsoi sipped at a glass of white wine. His legs hurt him a little but he had no desire to dull his perception any more than necessary. "I still can't believe it," Humphrey Hodges said.

"Believe it!" Borsoi smiled. "But now we must capitalize on it. With Roman Makowski in the White House—once he gets down out of that damned airplane—we have an edge. If we can destroy the Patriots, one day everyone in this miserable excuse for a nation will awaken and find out that the war is over and somehow they lost. Exactly what we want. Makowski will fire Rudolph Cerillia, the Patriots' short-lived alliance with the FBI will come to an end, and they will never recover without Holden. It was only a matter of time until Holden became a national leader for the Patriots, coordinated Patriot efforts against us on a national basis, began to win, perhaps. But with Holden gone, that bitch Rose Shepherd will never be able to take over overall command, although she is at least as qualified as Holden is. But she's a woman, and the demographics of the Patriot organizations nationwide make her ascendancy impossible. And, in any event, she will probably be taken or killed. So—our problems will be solved, won't they?"

"I guess," Hodges said rather lamely. Borsoi wondered sometimes why he didn't just kill the man and be done with it. "But what if—"

"If Holden doesn't come? He has to, of course. He will know through his sources—likely that radio fellow—"

"Lem Parrish," Hodges supplied.

"Yes. Or someone else we may not even be aware of—but Holden will know that Steel's entire FBI unit is hospitalized, will know that the FLNA has every intention of using the second missile battery, will know he is the only hope to stop the FLNA. So he will not be able to resist. He will come in full force to recapture the missiles and, when he does . . ." Borsoi sipped again at his wine. "That will be that. I must admit, I am looking forward to meeting him again if he can be taken alive." He thought about his legs as he lit a cigarette.

Lem Parrish's good right hand was inside the pocket of his sport coat, his fingers folded around the butt of the Smith & Wesson. It was one of those tiny revolvers with the built-in hammer shroud, stainless steel. He thought the name was particularly appropriate tonight: Bodyguard.

He saw movement in the doorway of the apartment building at the end of the block, but with the streetlights shot out or broken and no light except for the light from the few windows without drawn curtains, it was hard to be certain if it was Butch or just some bum lying in a doorway for shelter in the night.

But then he saw the movement again. The strong, by-now-familiar limp, the old slouch hat, the hands in the pockets. Butch Sidowski was a resourceful man. He was an informant to the police and, to double dip, since there was no second police department to go to, he went to newsmen and media people who would pay for the same information. Since the coming of the FLNA, things had been hard for Butch. He could no longer go to the police because, in his own words, "Don't trust who's honest no more." He lived off what he begged, stole, or the information he sold to the press.

He had called the station. "Lem?"

"Butch—good to hear from you, but not now. See—"

"Lem. There was two of them missile things. I know where the other one is. The usual." And the phone line had clicked dead.

Lem Parrish didn't trust phone lines, particularly his own, and even though the usual meeting place and time was known only to him and to Butch Sidowski, there was always the chance of being followed. Or what if somebody had gotten to Butch? Threatened to beat him? But that had been done lots of times, his nose and twisted fingers testimony to that. What else did you do to a man like Butch short of killing him? And that made Sidowski's information so reliable, because he was beneath contempt, he was above dishonor.

Lem Parrish had taken the bulb out of the dome light of the Mercedes weeks ago and didn't plan on replacing it, at least not until the FLNA was gone. It made a person too good a target. He stepped out of the car onto the street, the door open, his keys still in the ignition, the parking brake off.

Butch Sidowski, for all his shortcomings, was as patriotic and American as they came, and he hated the FLNA. Lem Parrish considered that for a moment.

Maybe some of the hatred stemmed from his loss of income since their arrival.

Sidowski stopped beside the front bumper. He never liked to stand too close to anyone. Apparently he was acutely aware that he reeked of cheap booze and body odor.

"How you doing, Butch? I didn't mean to try to put you off on the phone, but this has been hell today."

"I been watchin' on the TV at the shelter." He had a curious way of accentuating the letter *T* and it made the inflection of his words come out all wrong.

"How do you know about a second launcher?"

"I heard people talkin'. Some of them scumbag gangbanger shits like the FLNA use to do their fuckin' dirty work. They thought they was hot stuff knowin' about it and where it was bein' stashed and all. I just did like I usually do and listened while they figured I was too dirty to roll and too drunk to care. I don't even want money for this one, Lem."

Lem Parrish was taken aback. "Why not?"

"I got pride, man. You just make sure when the Patriots nail 'em, they make it nice and noisy so it gets on the TV and I can see all about it, okay?"

"Okay. *If* I meet any Patriots." Lem Parrish smiled. It had come to be a running joke between them, the thing about the Patriots. It wasn't that Lem Parrish distrusted Butch Sidowski, but when Sidowski would drink, how was anybody to know what he would say. "Where, Butch?"

Butch walked a little closer and what little wind there was seemed suddenly to shift. Parrish coughed, wanted to turn away, but wouldn't because he would have embarrassed Sidowski. "You and me go way back, Lem. Make

sure they know. For what those shits did. Just make sure
the Patriots know, huh?"

"All right." Parrish nodded, defeated totally by Butch
Sidowski's sincerity. "I'll make sure."

"That little airport—north of the city, ain't it?"

"What airport?"

Butch smiled sheepishly, his stubbled chin distending
as his right hand rubbed at it. "Camp Fort Field, huh?"

"Camp Fort Field. That's up in Harrison County."

"Search me." Butch shrugged. "But they got it there,
Lem."

Parrish let go of his gun, started to dig in his right
trouser pocket for his money clip, held the bills with the
stumps of the fingers of his left hand. He looked up as
Butch said, "Remember what I told ya?"

"From one friend to another, then?" Parrish almost
pleaded with the old man to take some money in ex-
change for his information.

"Just get them bastards and I'm paid enough, huh?"
Sidowski just grinned. "But I'll take a cigarette."

Lem Parrish put away his cash and started digging in
his pockets again.

David Holden sat beside the CB base station. Mitch
Diamond was on the other end, reading a series of numbers. Rosie Shepherd was transcribing them by hand onto
a steno pad balanced on her lap, and Pete Villalobos was
copying them onto a battery-operated boom box tape recorder. ". . . nineteen, four, seventy-three, twenty-two,
one hundred and five, sixty-two, four, nineteen . . ."

Holden looked over Rose's shoulder at the pad while
simultaneously looking at the specially prepared grid
map of the state. Odd numbers were lines of latitude or
degrees thereof, even digits were longitudinal references.

The code consisted of using the first letter of the town name (based on position dot), which appeared inside the finely drawn grid squares. When there was more than one town or municipality, the town with the largest population was the key. Assembling the letters spelled out the message.

The numbers stopped, then Diamond's voice came back, "Got it?"

Rosie took up the microphone. "That's a big ten-four. Thanks."

"Right. Out."

David Holden began the deciphering in earnest. . . .

Geoffrey Kearney lit a cigarette. When he was in America, he always smoked Pall Malls because they tasted so good. But he smoked very few cigarettes. Long ago he'd decided that the very polluted air that he breathed as a citizen of Earth was vastly more carcinogenic so, when he smoked, he didn't waste time feeling guilty, he simply enjoyed the sensation. A Metro police official named Kaminsky—a rather disagreeable-looking fellow, balding with beedy little eyes—and an FBI official who hadn't offered his name sat together at a small wooden table in the interrogation room. Kearney was about to ask them if he was under arrest or this was merely a friendly chat.

"Mr. Kearney, just exactly what do you do with the Mounties?" Kaminsky asked, tapping a pencil against the tabletop for emphasis.

He hadn't liked this Kaminsky chap from the first so he decided to have a little fun with him. "Well, if you promise not to spread it about, you see, when the Mountie service began there was no provision made against color blindness as a disqualification for duty. It's my job—a tough one, but someone has to do it—to make certain that the color-blind Mounties are wearing their red coats instead of some other color."

The FBI man laughed.

The twitty-looking fellow, Kaminsky, looked as if he half believed it; the situation seemed promising. "But in all seriousness, I'm chief training officer for the RCMPETCTRT." The FBI man was smiling again, but Kaminsky was apparently taking it all in.

"A counterterrorist specialist, eh? What do those initials stand for?" Kaminsky insisted.

Kearney looked from side to side, walked over to the door, heard the scrape of a chair behind him, peered through the small wire-reinforced window set at chin level and into the empty hallway outside the interrogation room. Then he looked back toward the table. Kaminsky was standing now. "RCMPETCTRT is very hush-hush. Only a select handful know the true mission. Do both of you have your CIA's Triad Eight Clearance?"

The FBI fellow was almost falling out of his chair, but the disagreeable Kaminsky was soaking it all in like a sponge.

"No?" Kearney said, breaking the silence. "Well, I suppose under the circumstances—but I must swear you to secrecy."

"I swear to secrecy." Kaminsky nodded soberly.

The FBI man, stifling a laugh, said, "Ohh, me too."

"All right then. RCMPETCTRT stands for Royal Canadian Mounted Police—are you sure I should say this?"

Kaminsky nodded vigorously, his little eyes positively gleaming, the top of his head almost blindingly bright.

"Well, then." Kearney nodded, lowering his voice to a conspiratorial whisper. "Royal Canadian Mounted Police

Extraterrestrial Counterterrorist Reaction Team. We're fighting creatures from outer space, gentlemen."

The FBI man broke out laughing.

Ralph Kaminsky looked as if he'd bitten his tongue and just as unhappy as if he had.

"I don't want you going with me on this," David told her.

Rose Shepherd put her left arm through the loop made by the shoulder harness of the white plastic Ken Null rig for her Model 60 Smith. He helped her with the cross-over strap and she pulled it over her right shoulder, then wrapped it to her belt. She snapped it shut. "I'm going. Period, David."

"We're doing this too fast. We have zip intelligence about the area because the FLNA never does anything up there in the mountains. Have you ever been to Camp Fort Field?"

She had to admit "No."

"Well, none of us have. We're going to have to go in there, do a quick blind recon, and then hit wherever they've got the missile launcher."

"It's too bad Steel and his guys are in the hospital."

"At least they're all alive." David nodded. He opened her purse and took a cigarette from the pack inside, lit it with her lighter.

She smiled at him. If she thought about him enough, she honestly could feel her nipples hardening. And, considering that she wasn't wearing a bra because of the laceration to her shoulder, she tried to avoid thinking about him so that her T-shirt wouldn't tell any tales. "So —what'll we do with it when we get it back—the missile thing, I mean?"

"Well, ahh—we give it back to the army. I mean, it's

no use to us unless the FLNA starts using tanks or armored cars. And we don't blow up office buildings, Rosie —damn them!"

"I have faith," Rose told him, watching his eyes, liking the way they watched her back. It was warm, but pleasantly so, in the tent. The nights had suddenly gotten colder and it was fun to hide under a blanket with David. Nipples, she reminded herself. "I have faith that the President will pull out of it." In the yellowish light of the Coleman lamp, David looked less sure than she. "I really do. How could this country survive an ass like this Makowski? The President will pull out of the coma and take charge again. I know he will."

"Look, ahh—maybe, ahh—maybe he'll rise to the occasion, huh? Makowski, I mean; the presidency can do things like that to a man. Look at some of the vice presidents who turned into great—"

It was history lecture time, and she actually enjoyed David's in-depth knowledge of a subject she'd never really understood that well, or liked. She'd even found herself starting to read some of David's books, starting to listen every time someone began talking about something that touched on history. And maybe that was what was wrong with America, people not being in touch with their history any more.

"Look, David. Cerillia'll be fired and we'll be right back where we started, won't we?"

"No—how can Makowski fire a presidential appointee when the President is still alive? There's never been an acting President, for God's sake. Even when Ike was having heart attacks and Nixon wound up running the country, it was still a vice president filling in for the President. If the Vice President was still alive, this wouldn't be happening at all."

"Maybe he'll just be such a little shit that Congress'll impeach him—Makowski, I mean."

"His party controls Congress," David told her. She knew that, but still, weren't most of the men in Congress Americans first underneath their party loyalties? "Anyway, the stuff Makowski talks about is pretty much the stated position of his party. Raise taxes to pay for a welfare state, be soft on criminals, distrust the intelligence of the electorate. Makowski could be the greatest asset the FLNA ever had. He can bankrupt the country while giving the FLNA an easier time of it."

"I think the President'll get well," she said again. Rose Shepherd wiggled her toes before stepping into her combat boots. She prayed the President would get well.

Roman Makowski sat at the President's desk—his desk now. There were television monitors, phones in several different colors, a rack of buttons on a console with which he could call any one of the aides aboard *Air Force One.* He decided to try that.

He punched for the direct line to the cockpit. "Pilot?"

"Yes, Mr. President?"

"Take us down. There's a country that needs tending."

"But—"

"Take us down." He wasn't worried about sneak attacks. He was worried about running out of time to get things done. He had no worry that the President whom the American people had elected would come out of his coma. The doctors were almost a hundred percent certain that he would never wake up. But there was a country to mold.

First on his list was Rudolph Cerillia. Already he was having a statement prepared that expressed his condolences to the family of the Vice President, expressed his sympathy to the First Lady concerning the President's condition. He wondered, almost absently, if he could declare martial law in the wake of the attack on the security conference. And that statement—he stared out the window at the unremitting cloud layers. They were tinged with gold. That statement would express his grave doubts over the efficacy of security procedures at the conference. Had the very procedures themselves invited disaster? He was directing the Congress to appoint a special prosecutor to determine culpability and, until the investigation was concluded, he would ask FBI Director Cerillia to step down temporarily.

Much to do to mold a country. All of it would take time, and there was no time like the present.

CHAPTER

19

It was new to them, using video as a means of reconnaissance. But the equipment had sort of happened into their hands and David Holden had seen its potential.

He watched the monitors as the two cameras panned over the airfield, one from either side of the Cessna Pete Villalobos had piloted.

At the far end of the field there was a solitary hangar, large enough for several good-sized aircraft, large enough too for an eighteen-wheeler carrying a half-track-mounted antitank guided missile launcher battery. Two small planes were parked near the hangar, one a single-engine like the Cessna, the other a twin-engine Beechcraft. "That's an E fifty-five, I think," the usually taciturn Villalobos remarked over Holden's shoulder. "Good plane."

There were three cars parked at the side of the hangar, and as the Cessna made its second sweep of the runway, one of the cameras picked up the cars in greater detail. Each was a four-door sedan, capable of carrying six men.

The video cut out at the end of the second pass. Any

more passes would call undue attention to the plane's mission. There was no ground reconnaisance.

Rose lit a cigarette, offered one to Holden. Holden took it, tasting her lipstick after she lit it for him. "How many guys—eighteen or twenty?" Rosie asked.

"At least twenty." Holden nodded, exhaling smoke through his mouth and nostrils. "If we're overestimating, wonderful. But we'll figure on a minimum of twenty guys and, under the circumstances, a maximum of twice that number. They'll be watching their missiles really carefully. Considering wounded and leaving some people to guard the camp, how many can we muster, Rosie?"

Rose seemed to be running numbers in her head, then smiled as she said, "Including me, thirty-six."

He smiled back. "All right," Holden whispered.

Pete Villalobos held the Cessna's yoke in his fingertips as effortlessly as a commuter might hold the steering wheel of a station wagon. Holden had flown planes like this before, knew the procedures as Villalobos reduced airspeed, gliding the Cessna down onto the single runway.

There was a bump, a barely noticeable lurch, and the plane was taxiing toward the hangar at the opposite end of the field. David Holden reached under his right thigh to the full-size Beretta 92F there, loosening his seat restraint and leaning slightly forward, his left hand bracing him against the cockpit dash. He slipped the larger of the two Beretta 9mms he habitually carried under his tweed sport coat into the waistband of his trousers at the small of his back, positioned the butt properly, and leaned back against the seat.

Under his left armpit was the second Beretta, the 92F Compact; under his right armpit were two twenty-round

93R extension magazines and the Defender knife in its inverted sheath.

As Villalobos brought the Cessna to a stop and cut the engine, Holden looked at him. Villalobos zipped closed the bottom of his bomber jacket to cover the butt of the .45 Colt Government model in his belt, then gave a silent nod.

Villalobos opened his door and Holden followed him out, dropping to the tarmac.

Holden looked toward the hangar. His battle plan was simple. Get to the hangar and create as much havoc as he could until Rose led in the two groups of Patriots on both sides of the hangar. They were already within twenty yards of the runway border.

Rose had told him, "This is damn stupid, David. If it's gotta be this way, fine, but—"

"Who should I send? What do I say? 'I'm important; you're not. So go get yourself killed maybe'? No. You wouldn't say that either. Moment Pete and I get through that front door, you and your people close in. We play it right and you're on your toes, I won't be inside more than thirty, maybe forty-five seconds. Not enough time for anything to happen."

She had always told him he was a poor liar; she was right. Forty-five seconds was enough time for anything to happen.

As he and Villalobos moved toward the hangar, Holden said loudly, "If there's nobody here, we're shit outa luck, Pete."

"You're telling me?" Villalobos would have made a lousy actor. "With the way the oil pressure is falling, we probably won't get back off the ground—man." The last word came as almost an afterthought, as if Villalobos had suddenly remembered the rest of his speech or something. Which, in fact, Holden realized, was exactly the case.

"Let's check in here," Holden said, stopping to look at the hangar and pointing toward the door. "If anybody's around this airfield, maybe we can at least find a scrap of hose to get us airborne again."

David Holden doubted that such actors as Sir Laurence Olivier or Sean Connery would have been quaking in their boots over the competition their dialogue delivery might present; but, on the plus side, the average FLNA-er wasn't gifted at dramatic criticism, could barely read well enough to handle his own birth certificate, and was too stupid to care.

They stopped before the human-size entry door to the hangar. "Let's check it out inside, Pete," Holden said.

"Okay!" Villalobos responded with unnecessary enthusiasm.

Holden glanced at his watch as he reached for the door handle with his left hand, his right hand near the front of his coat.

He turned the knob.

He stepped into a small anteroom about the size of a bathroom. It was well lighted. "Stay outside," he hissed to Pete. The deal with Rosie was that once both he and Pete were inside the hangar, she should come running with the rest of the Patriots.

Holden drew the larger Beretta and reached up under his left armpit with his left hand to rip the smaller Beretta free. The door beyond had no knob and looked as if it would swing inward when pushed.

David Holden took a half step back, kicked at the door, and rasped, "Pete!"

As Holden angled through the door, running in a low

crouch, he could barely see anything. It was as if he had walked into a fog.

Something assailed his nostrils and his lungs burned.

Movement. Another door opening. Men in gas masks with automatic weapons. Holden gagged, stumbled, fell to his knees, raising both pistols. As he looked up, his eyes streaming tears, he saw a video camera, then another and another. Holden fired, one of the gas-masked men going down, then another. He jumped to his feet, running, his lungs feeling as if they were on fire, his eyes so clouded with tears he could barely see. Pete Villalobos stepped inside the room. Automatic weapons fire came from behind Holden, and Villalobos went down. Holden wheeled toward the sound, losing his balance, regaining it, sagging against the wall, firing his pistols, killing a man in a gas mask, an M-16 assault rifle falling to the building floor.

From outside he could hear gunfire.

Hands reached for him. Holden stabbed the muzzle of the Beretta toward the body belonging to the hands and saw another face behind a gas mask. He fired into the chest twice; the body rocked back, dead.

Holden was to the door. Pete Villalobos, eyes streaming tears from the gas, reached up to him. Holden thrust a Beretta into his trouser band, grabbed Villalobos's right arm, and hauled his friend to his feet.

He had him. Now he twisted Pete's body toward the swinging door. It wouldn't budge. There was no handle.

David Holden, clutching both pistols, held Villalobos upright beside him. Concentrated chemical Mace fogged the interior of the building. His face and hands burned with it.

More gunfire came from outside the hangar.

"Rosie," Holden choked.

* * *

Rose Shepherd sprayed her M-16 into the loft door from which the machine guns were firing. The opening, thirty feet above the runway surface and square over the main hangar doors, commanded a view of the entire airfield.

The men and women with her were going down, caught in a killing zone.

The hangar doors opened.

Rose Shepherd threw herself behind the near one, against the wall. Half a dozen other Patriots did the same. Eight of her people were down, some dead.

There was a roaring sound from inside the hangar. Rose changed magazines, the M-16 in her right hand, the Glock-17 pistol with a nineteen-round extension magazine in her left.

They had to get inside the hangar.

"Follow me! Inside!" She broke around the door, firing as soon as she cleared it.

A helicopter, already airborne, the pilot very good she realized on one level of consciousness, flying a mere few feet above the concrete, straight toward her and the open doors. She started to fire again. As the helicopter spun on its axis, she saw the nose bubble. Spread-eagled over it, lashed there somehow, was David Holden.

"David!"

She couldn't shoot.

The chopper was coming straight for her. She threw down the M-16 and the Glock pistol, running toward the helicopter as it passed her and reaching for it. The helicopter was through the open doors now and starting to climb.

She hurled her body toward the runners, had her

hands on one. As the helicopter surged upward, her fingers slipped.

She fell, hitting the tarmac hard, the wind knocked from her.

Unable to rise, her throat and lungs aching, she cried, "David!"

Rose Shepherd's eyes filled with tears.

The machine guns had been operated electronically.

When Rose began scouring the interior of the hangar for Pete Villalobos, she walked into the gas chamber and immediately began to cry again, coughing, lungs burning.

Using her torn BDU blouse, soaked with water, over her face and holding her breath as much as she could, she reentered the gas chamber with three other Patriots. Both her knees were skinned and bleeding, and she leaned on Patsy Alfredi to walk.

She almost tripped over Pete Villalobos.

He was dead, several bullet wounds in his chest and abdomen, his throat slit ear to ear.

They covered Pete's body, coughing and choking and crying as they moved on. The gas chamber had been built at the side of the hangar. It was clearly a trap. Whoever passed the information that brought them here would pay, but only after she got David back. Rose told herself that he was still alive.

They found David's Beretta 9mms, both of them shot out, slides locked back over empty magazines. The handguns were just a few feet from Pete Villalobos's body.

There was a door leading from the front of the hangar, opening inward only, without a handle or knob. The door was sealed with a multilayer rubber and cloth gasket.

When she could no longer breathe, Rose Shepherd left the gas chamber and sat outside in the wind, shivering, trembling with rage. David's pistols were on the runway surface beside her. "They knew it," she said simply to Patsy Alfredi. "They set this whole thing up. The missiles were just bait to get David, kill him or take him alive." She began to cough, choking, afraid to rub the tears from her eyes lest she rupture blood vessels. "Whoever passed this location along . . . I'm gonna find the mother-fucker and kill him. We've gotta find David." She stared at Patsy, who was kneeling beside her.

"Well—where would they take him? If he is still alive, where would they take him? Not to kill him, but maybe—"

"Get him to name names of Patriots, put together a damn hit list, maybe talk about the deal with Cerillia, use this to bring Cerillia down. They'll hold him hostage, maybe for the Patriots to close down. God Almighty." Rose Shepherd felt new tears, not from the gas but from the realization that David was lost to her. "I won't!" And she stood up, her knees hurting her, her trouser legs wet with her own blood. "I won't!" She shouted it toward the overcast sky in the direction the helicopter had flown. "You hear me!" Rose screamed. "Fuckin' hear me, you bastards! You're not gettin' him! You're not! I'll get him back!"

She sank down to her knees despite the pain, still unable to rub her eyes, looking at the sky. "David," she whispered, just letting the tears come hard and stream down along her cheeks. "David."

CHAPTER
20

He was instantly aware of every muscle in his body. His eyes would barely open. Through the slits of his eyelids, everything was blurred. It hurt even to look through the slits, hurt like no pain he had ever endured.

As David Holden tried to move, he felt a sound coming from deep inside him that was like a sound an animal might make, an animal that was in terrible agony. The sound was like something heard from inside a seashell picked up at the beach, hollow and very distant and unreal. There was a roaring sound, like wind. His ears were alive with pain.

His hands did not move. Nothing really moved.

He was cold, yet his skin felt as if it were on fire.

He shook; the world around him shook.

He tried to scream and the scream died inside of him.

The helicopter landed.

On his crutches, Dimitri Borsoi stood fewer than ten yards from it, the downdraft of the rotor blades whipping at his hair.

David Holden.

David Holden's body was shackled at wrists and ankles to the nose of the helicopter.

Holden's clothing was in tatters. His face was deeply bruised.

His full body weight hung from his wrists. His mouth was open, the almost imperceptible rising and falling of his chest the only testimony to his being alive.

Humphrey Hodges stood beside Borsoi. "Mr. Johnson. Please. He's a human being. Do something."

Dimitri Borsoi smiled at Hodges. "I intend to. I duly intend to."

CHAPTER
21

Mimi Baker had helped. It was the same blond wig that Rose Shepherd had worn when she'd disguised herself as a nurse, when she'd first met Luther Steel and the deal with the FBI was first discussed. She considered the irony of that; she was going to meet with Rudolph Cerillia and beg him to do something, even though the alliance was nearly at an end, the deal soured.

It had been like something out of one of those silly movies where college girls lived together in dormitories and swapped clothes and jewelry, borrowed each other's slips and shoes. It was imperative that she not be recognized during one of the random police searches. But it was equally imperative that she speak with Rudolph Cerillia personally. He had seemed eager to speak with her.

That scared her a little.

But, with Mimi Baker's help, she'd been given what was euphemistically called a makeover—more makeup than she normally used in a week on her face, cheekbones highlighted, eyes accentuated, even fake fingernails (her own were short because she was always breaking them on a gun or something else).

A pillow and a girdle, the pillow sewn onto it, making her look pregnant. Then the clothes. Several of the women at the Patriot encampment had recently had or were having babies, and there was no shortage of maternity clothes. Pants were ruled out because it would be too easy to tell that the baby wasn't a baby at all, only a pillow. Another woman's bra, heavily padded to fit. Then a borrowed pair of black flats. After Rose tried on several borrowed dresses, Mimi had pronounced, "That's you!" Rose Shepherd didn't agree but was tired of playing dress-up and wanted to see Cerillia. A blue dress that had enough room in it for two people, with one of those huge sailor collars that seemed to be a staple of maternity wear. A purse that matched the shoes.

And no gun.

She couldn't risk being pegged as a Patriot, and so many of the police in Metro knew her by sight anyway.

Terrified, she drove a borrowed Ford station wagon toward the northwestern suburbs. There were two police roadblocks.

She passed through both of them.

And now, massaging at the small of her back as some of the women had suggested she do, she stood in the lobby of the small office building, waiting. She had been waiting for ten minutes, according the little gold-colored borrowed Timex.

She started to fish in her purse for her cigarettes, but remembered that pregnant women didn't usually smoke these days. Her belly sweated with the pillow over it, and the girdle that held the pillow in place felt like an itchy rubber band around her midsection.

At last the elevator doors beyond the reception desk opened. A man she didn't recognize stepped out and looked about the foyer.

"Are you looking for me?" Rose Shepherd asked tentatively.

He looked at her oddly. "I was told to look for a Mrs. Cunningham."

"I'm Mrs. Cunningham."

He did a classic double take.

"I'm Mrs. Cunningham," she repeated, walking slowly toward him.

He shrugged his shoulders, waited beside the open elevator doors, and followed her inside, then used a key that was already in place to close the doors and start the elevator upward. "He told me you were a brunette. And he didn't mention anything about you being—"

"Very rapid pregnancy. And I dyed my hair." She nodded.

"Yeah."

The elevator stopped. There was no floor marking. He used the key and the door opened.

She stepped out, clutching her handbag over her pillow-stuffed abdomen.

"This way, ma'am."

He gestured toward a wooden door with no name, no number on it. He knocked on the door and the door opened. This time there was a man with an Uzi. "This isn't—"

"Tell Rudolph Cerillia I'm here. Let's stop screwin' around and wasting everybody's time, guys." She started through the doorway, the man with the Uzi stepping back, evidently not quite sure what to do with a pregnant lady. Pregnancy had its advantages, she decided, and a real kid had to beat a sweat-soaked pillow any day.

"Mr. Cerillia!" she called toward the door at the other side of the outer office.

After a second or so the door opened. Rudolph Cerillia

stood in the doorway, his left temple bandaged, one arm in a sling. "Mrs. Cunningham?"

Rose Shepherd forced a smile. "Don't tell me you didn't recognize me." Then she patted her abdomen, adding "After all we've meant to each other."

The FBI man with the Uzi dropped his jaw. She looked at him and said, "You'll catch flies that way."

"Come inside," Cerillia said.

She walked in as he held the door, took a few steps inside the room, and waited while he closed the door.

"Should I offer you a chair, Detective Shepherd?"

She leaned on the edge of the desk as she turned to look at him. "I need your help."

He looked away from her. "I can't help anybody, Detective. Catch the news? I've been asked to step down temporarily while my supposed laxity in matters concerning security for the conference is investigated. And then there's the matter of my alleged involvement with the Patriots. If I say now that I was acting under presidential orders, who's to back me up? The President could pass away at any moment. It's almost certain he'll never regain consciousness. Luther? Why should I destroy his career, his life? I'll take the heat, and though it wasn't fair to say there's nothing I can do to help you, there is very little. Are you sure Professor Holden is alive?"

"I feel it inside of me," Rose Shepherd almost whispered.

Cerillia smiled. "All right. But if we haven't been able to penetrate the FLNA in all this time, or find some central headquarters beyond Cedar Ridge Islands, I don't have any fresh ideas for finding Professor Holden."

"What about Charlie Lang? Wouldn't he know something?" She felt foolish asking the question, knew Cerillia's answer almost before he said it.

"Nothing that would help. If the FLNA is planning on holding Dr. Holden rather than immediately executing him, then they would certainly have picked a location Charlie Lang wouldn't be privy to, wouldn't they?"

"Yes." She exhaled so hard the padding in her bra shifted. She scooted up into a full sitting position on the end of the desk, letting her legs swing.

"You need swollen ankles, Detective."

"What?"

"As a finishing touch to your disguise. Pregnant women frequently have minor circulatory problems that bring about swollen ankles."

"I'll get padded stockings next time." She nodded. "We've gotta do something."

"Have you tried the source?"

"The informant? I checked with Lem Parrish. The informant was a man named Butch Sidowski. I know Butch. He's a street person, a bum. He wouldn't sell out to the FLNA for all the booze and cigarettes in the world. The information had to have been dropped on him by the gangbangers Lem said Butch overheard it from. And Butch is dead. Somebody ran him over with a truck. Twice."

"That kind of dead." Cerillia nodded soberly. "I'll see if I can get my people—who used to be my people—to try Lang if you think there's a chance. It's always worth a shot, I guess," he said, sounding more discouraged than she did, she thought.

"I've got another idea. These FLNA. Their bosses are all probably guys like that creep Borsoi/Johnson, right? Foreign?"

Cerillia looked at her, seemed to consider her words, then nodded slightly. "Most likely. But if you're thinking the CIA or one of the other agencies in the intelligence community can help, they wouldn't touch me with a ten-foot pole right now."

"No. You ever hear of a man named Thomas Ashbrooke?" Rose asked.

Cerillia sat down, seemed to think for a moment. "The name Ashbrooke rings a bell; something to do with the events of the last several months."

"He's David's father-in-law, Elizabeth Holden's father. David was telling me about him, showed me a note from him. He used to be into smuggling, gun running, things like that. He lives in Switzerland. He's rich. Maybe money can help," Rose offered.

"You want me to have him found, set up a means for contact between you?"

"Can you?" Rose asked him, shifting her fake baby a little. The girdle was killing her.

"And what then?"

"David's not dead. I gotta find him. There's nothing else so important. Without David, the Patriots around Metro'll fall apart. Sure, there'll still be some of us until we get croaked or caught, but David turned us into what we are. And without David's exploits against the FLNA sneaking into the news every once in a while and working through the Patriots' underground communications system, a lot of other Patriot cells in other cities'll start to wither away too. You need him."

"Miss Shepherd?" He smiled as he stood up. "I'll tell you something." Cerillia walked over toward the desk and reached out, as if he wanted to take her hand. She let him hold her hand. He said, "I know you love him. And it's kind of refreshing—these days especially—to see that kind of relationship, especially after all that's happened. So I don't know what I can do." Cerillia patted the back of her hand for emphasis, almost as if he were trying to revive her or something. "But whatever I can do, I will do. Now, tell me everything you can think of about this Thomas Ashbrooke and I'll get some wheels in motion. And I will check with Charlie Lang's interrogators. And I'll try pulling some other strings too. If I can help get him back for you—God help me for saying this—maybe the two of you would be better off getting out of the country. A man like David could be just as effective—in some ways more so—as an ex-Patriot, a figurehead to be looked up to."

"What are you saying?" Rose Shepherd asked, letting him hold her hand still but sliding off the end of the desk, standing.

Cerillia's eyes were hooded beneath the lids for a moment, then he looked her square in the eye. "If the President does die, as predicted, then Roman Makowski may run this country for quite a few years. He'll turn it into the little socialist paradise he's always wanted it to be. People like you, the majority of Americans, won't stand for that. There'll be a civil war that'll make this FLNA thing look mild by comparison. Mark my words." She hated that expression, its ominousness. "So I'll try to get David back because you love him and because this country may need him vastly more than you suspect, Miss Shepherd. Vastly more."

It was the one thing she'd always hated about being a woman. There was your menstrual cycle, which always came at the wrong time; there were public toilets in sleazo restaurants; there was having to shave your legs when you were already late for work. But as the tears welled up in her eyes, the thing she hated the most was that she couldn't stop them.

CHAPTER
22

"Dr. Holden? Can you hear me?"

David Holden thought for a moment that he was blind, because as he opened his eyes, he could see nothing at all. But as he inhaled, he felt the fabric against his mouth, felt it suck up against his face. There was a hood or something over his head. He tried to shake it away, but as he moved his head spasms of pain shook him.

He was cold.

His hands and feet were numb. They wouldn't move.

"Do you have any idea who I am?"

Holden tried to talk, but his throat was so dry he could not. His lips felt too large for his mouth.

The hood was ripped away and he squinted against the light, his eyes burning.

A bare bulb swung over his head as he opened his eyes again. He looked down across his body. His clothes were ripped. His shoes were gone and so were his socks. He was sitting. He couldn't move his legs or his arms. Tied?

He squinted harder to look past the swinging bulb and into the half shadow beyond.

The voice came again and he could see an outline,

nothing more. "I have been waiting for this opportunity. But like many opportunities, the reality of life interferes. You may wonder what I mean, Dr. Holden. Well, my meaning will be clear in a moment." The voice was even, almost pleasant, tinged a little with something reminiscent of insanity.

It went on. "For quite some time you were an annoying abstraction, nothing more. I wanted you dead the same way an animal in the field might want a bothersome fly dead because it incessantly buzzed at his ear. But that was all. I wanted you out of my life. And then we met. And after that I wanted more. You'll understand soon if you don't understand now. But I really wanted more. Death was not enough. But the exigencies of modern existence intrude. What is in your head is very valuable. The names of the Patriots who are in powerful positions in Metro and elsewhere, all the details of the agreement between the Patriots and FBI Director Cerillia. The location of your camps, the names of leaders of other Patriot cells. All of that. And so I am denied what I so hoped for. But there is a little time remaining to us."

David Holden tried to talk. Words didn't come.

"I confess that I must work within certain limits. For example, I cannot do to you what you did to me. It may be important at some date in the future that you be able to stand up, for example, look physically unharmed. Limitations. In a very short while for me, a very long while for you, you will be taken out of the country. It does not matter where, really. But far away from any help, any chance. And very talented people with very sophisticated techniques will make you willingly, cheerfully spill your guts, plead to tell them more. Perhaps you will be instrumental in our eventual victory here and elsewhere. Who can say? We may one day be colleagues. I understand that the techniques of my associates are very advanced. But for the few hours before your departure, I can do anything I wish to you so long as no permanent physical damage is done to your limbs or senses. I could, for example, do things to you that a man like you has never even considered possible for one human being to do to another. And I may. I intend to indulge myself, Doctor. At your expense, of course. And then you will be off, and the only time you will remember these few hours is when you awaken at night screaming from something that you will tell yourself was only a very bad dream. Think of me as a nightmare, Dr. Holden."

David Holden managed the word. "Who—"

"You do not recognize my voice. Well, there was little time for conversation when we met. The slut you fuck each night was in my care. I was about to drop her into the ocean. You were very heroic. We fought. I lost. But I didn't die. Both of my legs are broken, damage that I will soon enough recover from. You were very heroic when you saved your whore, Dr. Holden. Now the question is, how heroic are you really? Will you cry out? Will you scream? Show me how heroic you are, will you? I wish to be inspired."

David Holden's eyes were beginning to focus, the shape in the shadows becoming more distinct. A chair. Leaning beside it were two crutches.

It was Borsoi/Johnson. Holden remembered the face he had seen through the helicopter's Plexiglas, the almost satanic evil of it. He didn't need to see the face now. It was there, in his brain, would always be there.

"First I will tell you what I intend to do to you. We will move on to other activities as the seconds drag by for you. Do you have a strong heart? Because I would hate for you to die, Dr. Holden. You are a student of history.

Do you remember—can you tell me which Latin American dictator's secret police did pioneering work in the use of ice-cold water for nearly drowning a subject followed up by electric shock?" There was a pause. David Holden held his breath. "The technique is to use ice-cold water, immersing the subject's head until his lungs begin to burst and he is gulping the water. Then draw the victim out of the water, lay him flat on a cold slab, and beat his abdomen with boards in order to induce vomiting up of the water. Then, electrodes on leads from automobile storage batteries are attached to, well, certain sensitive areas. Say, the scrotum? Or the nipples of the breasts? How peculiar, humankind. Men having nipples." He laughed. "The tongue is a promising area. But then, after the electric shock, when the subject is worn beyond endurance, the drowning begins again. The fascinating aspect of the technique is its very inexorability. The subject realizes that the electric shock has ended but already knows the horror of the drownings and the beatings, and when these end the horror of the electric shock returns. Now, those are all the hints I will allow. Can you answer? Do you know who that dictator was? For twenty-five points, name that country if you can!"

David Holden said nothing. His body shook with cold and—he knew—with fear.

"Drowning first—and cheer up, Doctor. Perhaps the answer will come to you."

A hand knotted into David Holden's hair and he was ripped out of the chair, dragged a pace or two, then his head was plunged into a vat of water, ice cubes floating on its surface. He had barely enough time to gulp at air.

CHAPTER

23

Lionel Morrison loosed his seat restraint and folded down the tray table in front of him. Geoffrey Kearney lit a cigarette just as the "smoking permitted" light came on.

A man swayed a little as he walked down the portside aisle toward, Kearney assumed, the lavatory. A flight attendant was heading in the opposite direction. As she passed Kearney, she smiled at him.

"Pity this Borsoi fellow is dead. At least that would have given you a solid lead to follow," Morrison said abruptly.

Kearney was still watching the flight attendant. She had pretty legs. "You know, Inspector, I've always held to the theory that the fascination men have with women's legs has nothing to do with the legs at all. Rather what they lead up to. I always thought it a pity that the manufacturers did away with seams in women's stockings, that they were overlooking the obvious, how the eye followed the line made by the seam." He looked at Chief Inspector Morrison. "Either Borsoi—if even that's his real name—

is still alive, or he was never as important as the FBI assumed him to be. I'd gamble on the former."

"You think the fellow survived that fall into the ocean?"

"If he'd managed to stay afloat—how long can you tread water, Chief Inspector?"

"Well, I'm not that terribly keen on swimming, really, but I suppose for an hour or so if my life depended on it."

"Let's say Borsoi is a bit more keen on swimming than you. We also have to incorporate the likelihood that he sustained some rather nasty injuries in his fall. But let's say he could stay afloat by treading water and swimming, alternating to conserve his strength, realizing that nature was in his favor. He was only a few miles from shore. Disoriented, granted, but if he made these helicopter flights on a relatively regular basis he would have to have been a positive dolt not to memorize even subconsciously some of the coastal features, lights, things such as that. So, when he did the swimming part, we could safely assume that he would have swum in the correct direction more or less, certainly not out to sea. Working on that assumption, we mustn't forget nature—the tide."

The captain's voice came over the PA system, announcing how happy everyone was to have everyone aboard and the other usual things captains announced. Kearney extinguished his cigarette. A flight attendant— not the same one with the pretty legs but another one whose legs were almost as pretty—asked if they would like something from the beverage cart. Morrison took a whiskey, Kearney an American Chablis Blanc. As he poured and the flight attendants moved on, Kearney went on. "I consulted with several persons by telephone and came up with this. The tides are semidiurnal, which means roughly twelve hours and twenty-five minutes, or half a lunar revolution about the earth, between high-water periods. Calculating the approximate time of Borsoi's impromptu dip in the ocean, he would have gotten caught up in the high tide. In other words, rather than a neutral flow or a flow away from the shore, the tide would have aided him, drawing him in toward shore and facilitating his survival. Add to that—and this Borsoi must be a lucky chap—it was spring tide."

"Spring tide?" Morrison echoed.

"Fortnightly fluctuation in tidal levels. At spring tide the tides are higher. At neap tide, the other end of the pendulum, tides are lower. Lucky for Borsoi, spring tide would have exerted even more force to draw him in even more toward the shore. Say, for the sake of argument, that he broke a leg—a broken arm might well have done him in—and that the tide brought him ashore. What person, even these days, wouldn't help a stranger found injured on the beach? Borsoi, after all, can't be a dullard. He was probably decently dressed at the time, looked terrible and all, but with a glib tongue and once-decent clothes he was probably able to allay anyone's fears and get himself medical attention or whatever.

"My intention, Chief Inspector," Kearney continued, after pausing for a moment to sip at his wine, "is to gather up what I need and return to the coastal area off Cedar Ridge Islands and do some digging. Find whoever it was—if my theory is correct—who fished our friend out of the drink and track him from there. If that turns out a dead end, then I shall just have to think of something else. But working on the assumption Borsoi is still at the controls of the FLNA is my best option now."

"And if you do find this Borsoi fellow—then what?" Morrison asked, his voice lowering.

Geoffrey Kearney sipped again at his wine. "The inter-

ests of my government and yours might best be served by
his immediate demise, but then we'd never know what's
at the heart of all this, would we? Are our Soviet friends
preaching détente out of one side of their mouths or is
some unholy alliance we can't even imagine behind the
FLNA? If killing is the only way, then Borsoi will die.
But if I can use Borsoi to find his masters, everyone
might best be served. There's a charming Americanism
that's apropos, I think: I'll just 'play it by ear,' Chief
Inspector."

Kearney downed the rest of the wine in the plastic
glass.

CHAPTER
24

She sat up, cold and alone. Her face, her breasts, her abdomen, her thighs, they were slick with sweat.

Rose Shepherd stood up into a crouch, all the height of the tent would allow. Her T-shirt and panties were soaking. She looked at the time on her watch. Hours before dawn. And if she took a shower now, there would be nothing but cold water. She stripped out of her clothes.

The blanket she had used was wet as well, but there was a dry spot and she used that like a towel to dry her body. Then she cast it into a corner of the tent and took the other blanket. It still smelled of him. She wrapped it around her as she climbed back into the sleeping bag.

If Cerillia could provide no leads, what was she to do? She would never give up.

Or what if David were dead? She would never believe that until she saw his remains with her own eyes. His remains. Rose Shepherd shivered.

She rolled over onto her side, curling up into an almost fetal position, hugging the blanket around her, trying to stop shaking.

The fault was in herself. It was a dangerous plan and

she should never have let him try to carry it out. She had
been thinking with her body instead of her brain. He had
been trying to minimize casualties, never expected a trap.
And the FLNA still had that second launcher and at
least twelve guided missiles it could use at any time, anywhere. And it was all up to her now. Nobody would
search for David the way she would. Nobody would.

She couldn't fall asleep.

She would hound Cerillia until he came up with something, anything. Luther Steel would be out of the hospital
in a few days. Steel would help. Steel and the others in his
unit.

And suddenly she thought about Roman Makowski,
the almost self-proclaimed President. What if he kept
Cerillia on the hot seat and was able to effectively sabotage any chance for success against the FLNA?

What Cerillia had said to her haunted her. That if she
found David—"When," she corrected herself aloud—she
and David should leave the country, fight a political battle rather than fight the enemy here. She couldn't accept
that. Why should other people risk their lives while she
and David were safe?

She knew the answer to that and she pushed it away
from her. She would never be without him again, he
would always be with her, have his arms around her.

A civil war?

Cerillia had spoken about a civil war. But she couldn't
imagine the people of the United States fighting each
other. She rolled over, twisted up in the blanket, moving
her legs to get the blanket around her properly. And
Canada and Mexico were just as much under assault by
the FLNA. What would be their fate? Civil wars as well?

Rose Shepherd made herself believe in two things: The

President would somehow revive, kick Makowski out of his acting presidency, set things right again; and she would find David Holden. If she failed in that, nothing else would matter anyway.

CHAPTER

25

David Holden felt hands on him as he opened his eyes. It was starting again.

He'd passed out, he thought, not sure.

His vision was still blurred.

Hands and feet were meaningless terms to him. He couldn't even feel a sensation of numbness anymore.

Dragged.

He was naked, shivering.

The water.

Ice cubes floated in it.

He inhaled and his lungs ached.

His head was thrust down into the water.

There was a hand on the back of his neck, forcing his head farther down into the water. It was some sort of barrel, perhaps a fifty-gallon drum. There was an oily taste to the water, or was that only imagination? The hand on his neck pushed harder and harder. His lungs were exploding. He knew that. The pressure on his ears. Water up his nose. He could no longer keep his mouth closed, and the water flooded through him. He thought that his bowels loosened but then he was ripped from the water, thrown down on the floor, his head banging against the cold concrete. His body was racked with chills.

He saw a fleeting glimpse of Borsoi/Johnson. And then the boards moved downward. He was screaming and choking at the same time. The boards smashed across his abdomen as the water sprayed out of his raw throat and down across his body. They kept beating him until nothing came up and still his stomach heaved.

Hands.

The chair.

The storage batteries.

His mouth was forced open, a rubbery-tasting block put into his mouth.

He tasted the lead from the cable as it was clamped to his tongue.

Hands at his testicles.

He tried to scream but heard only a sound like something from an animal.

The electricity.

He fell out of the chair.

Someone touched him and swore. Then the rubber-gloved hands hauled him back up into the chair.

The electricity.

The pain started in his mouth and testicles and swept over him until it consumed him and his body vibrated with it, pulsed with it.

He fell out of the chair, writhed on the cement. The electricity was still coming.

Blackness.

Water.

He didn't hold his breath this time. He thought absently that maybe he was trying to die. Blackness.

Pain. The rawness of his throat awakened him as he vomited again.

To the chair.

Nipples and testicles.

He could no longer feel the pain.

David Holden lay on the cement floor. He didn't want to open his eyes.

"Dr. Holden? Have you thought of the name yet? Of the name of the country where this technique was initiated? Cat got your tongue, as they say?"

If he died, he would never be able to kill Borsoi.

They hauled him up. Somehow the electrodes had been disconnected from him. Before his head was shoved below the surface of the water, he inhaled as hard as he could.

He watched the Mercedes enter the driveway. He could see the driveway clearly from the window. Why had the chair been positioned there?

The Mercedes stopped.

Reefer went down into the driveway, spoke with the man getting out from behind the wheel.

Reefer and the second man started to enter the house. Borsoi turned his eyes toward the hallway, heard the door open and close. As he looked toward the hallway, his eyes passed the small table beside him. On it lay his cigarettes, a disposable lighter, an ashtray, and the shoulder holster taken from David Holden. Both guns Holden had used were left behind in the gas chamber. The holster was fitted with two twenty-round 9mm magazines and a curious-looking knife.

In the doorway of the living room stood Innocentio Hernandez. "Dimitri. It is good to see you."

"It is good to see you, Innocentio." Borsoi nodded.

There was a puzzled look on Reefer's face, due to, Borsoi assumed, Hernandez's use of Borsoi's real first name. "Mr. Johnson? You need anything?" Reefer asked.

"No, Reefer. Thank you." And he looked at Hernandez. "Innocentio?"

"You have a beer?"

"Yeah. Sure thing."

Reefer smiled, disappearing from the doorway as Hernandez crossed the room in three strides and sat on the couch facing Borsoi. Hernandez was a large man, but Borsoi seemed to notice it more, seated as he was. Hernandez was about six four, perhaps 250 pounds, with dark, curly hair, a clean-shaven face, and smiling eyes. He looked like a huge dark-skinned baby, Borsoi always thought.

Reefer returned with beer. Hernandez nodded affably as he took a swallow. He rolled the bottle in his hands as Reefer walked out of the room. "How is your guest?" Innocentio Hernandez asked, smiling good-naturedly.

"He is alive. That is all that was promised."

"You should not mix business with pleasure, *amigo.*" Hernandez laughed.

"But it was such pleasure." Borsoi smiled.

Hernandez shrugged his massive shoulders, his eyes twinkling. "He will not be any good if he cannot think anymore, huh? But what you did will work out, I think. With a little kindness"—he smiled, sipped at his beer—"and the memories of what you have done for him." He sipped at his beer again. "Well, he should be cooperative. A smart man, this professor?"

"Very intelligent, I think. I almost stopped a few times because I thought he would die. I hope you appreciate that."

"Oh, yes." Hernandez downed the rest of the beer and set the bottle on the floor beside his track shoe–clad feet. They were huge. "I am told that we will try to turn him, use him to denounce his government. It will make the Patriots lose some of their will and make the government come down harder on them. A stroke of good luck—huh?—this Makowski asshole coming to power."

"Umm." Borsoi nodded, noncommittal.

"Where is he?"

"Holden? In the garage. He is resting. Do you want me to have him put in your trunk?"

"Do you think an injection will kill him? I do not want him to awaken."

Borsoi considered that. "No. It should not. Pentathol?"

"Yes." Hernandez nodded. "What is that beside you?"

"It was Holden's," Borsoi said, glancing at the shoulder holster.

Hernandez stood up, approached Borsoi and the small table beside him. "May I?"

"Yes. Of course."

Hernandez picked up the shoulder holster. "A most interesting design, this. For the Beretta, huh? And what is this?" He drew the knife from the inverted sheath affixed to the double magazine pouches. "This is magnificent, this *cuchillo*." He laughed. "It says 'The Defender' on it, huh? Handmade?"

"I think so."

Hernandez fisted the knife, taking a swipe at an imaginary enemy with the gracefully styled Bowie-shaped blade. "This spine here," he said, pointing out to Borsoi the upper portion of the blade. "It could be sharpened to make this a full double edge. I like that. I know knives a great deal. This skull crusher at the butt—" He began to unscrew it, never finishing his sentence. He poured the contents of the hollow handle into his massive palm. "An extractor, a firing pin, firing pin spring, a set of grip screws. All for the Beretta 92F, I think. Headache pills! Ha! This Holden will need those, I think." He laughed again. "Waterproof matches. The standard things." He closed the butt cap. "This handle is most peculiar. It looks like it would be slick to hold, but it molds to the hand. *Esta bien*. How much do you take for this? The knife and the shoulder holster. I carry a Beretta some-times and I could use it, Dimitri."

Borsoi had considered the irony of keeping Holden's knife, using it as his own. But Innocentio was an old comrade and an important man. "It is my gift to you, Innocentio. Use it to fight the capitalists and I will be pleased."

"You are a fine fellow, Dimitri!" Hernandez exclaimed, resheathing the knife.

"Take good care of Professor Holden for me," Borsoi told him.

"You have my word for that, *amigo!*" And he laughed again.

CHAPTER
26

David Holden awoke.

He was warm, but not unpleasantly so.

He was lying in a bed, a light blanket over him. The room was well lighted with sunshine that filtered through the curtained windows.

He sat up, his muscles stiff. He looked at his body as he flipped back the covers. There were bruises on his chest and crotch. His tongue felt odd in his mouth. He spoke just to see if he still could. "Four score and seven years ago, our fathers brought forth on this continent a new nation, conceived in liberty and dedicated to the proposition that all men are created equal. . . ." He speech sounded normal enough to him.

He threw his legs over the side of the bed and felt more muscle pain and pain in his back as well. He stood up, then doubled over and fell to his knees, his stomach muscles knotting, the pain excruciating. He knelt there, sucking air, for he didn't know how long. Using the bed to support him, he tried to stand, more slowly this time. And this time he made it. He inhaled, stood, looked around the room.

On a chair beside the bed were some clothes. He examined them. They were not his but looked the right size and were clean. On the little table beside the bed was his Rolex. He slipped the bracelet over his left wrist, closed the Flip-Lock clasp. From the date shown on the watch, he was missing four days.

Cigarettes and a disposable lighter. He opened the pack, dropped the torn-off cellophane and foil into an empty wastebasket beside the table, then extracted one of the cigarettes. Winstons. Holden broke off the filter from one and lit the cigarette. He had to adjust the flame of the disposable lighter because it was high enough to use as a torch. He inhaled and coughed as he exhaled.

He walked to the window nearest him and looked out at a bright sun. Warm air came through the screen. Beyond the window there was a small garden, the flowers unrecognizable. Beyond the garden, a greensward, and beyond that, the grassy area extending for half the length of a football field, was a high hedgerow. He assumed there was a fence just beyond.

Holden walked across the room, a little light-headed from the cigarette. He tried the knob on his door. It turned. The door opened and he peered into what lay beyond—a corridor with tiled floor and stuccoed walls. A small table sat a few feet down from the doorway and about twice that distance from the head of a staircase. On the table was a flower arrangement. The flowers were fresh. He closed the door, leaned against it, trying to reconstruct the last few days.

The torture sessions. His body still bore the marks. His stomach muscles ached more than anything else, from the beatings with the boards. He was still black and blue under the hair.

There was a small doorway on the other side of the room. He walked toward it, then through it.

A bathroom. He lifted the lid on the toilet seat, dropped the cigarette butt into the bowl. Slowly he sat down. He was too tired to stand and expected that urinating would be an unpleasant experience after what he had endured. He was right; his muscles cramped on him as he tried and eventually succeeded.

He stood again, flushed, watching the water in the trap. There was something wrong.

He shook his head, stared at himself in the bathroom mirror. There was no four-day growth of beard on his face, but he needed a shave. He wasn't at all surprised that there was a razor; however, it was battery powered. He used it. A new toothbrush and toothpaste and mouthwash were on the sink. He used all three, found the dental floss and used that. He smiled. They weren't as smart as they thought, whoever they were.

Fresh towels were hung beside the shower and more were stacked on a little shelf on the wall. Inside the shower, tiled, well appointed, were bar soap, shampoo, even conditioner.

He decided to take a shower.

For the first few minutes he simply let the pleasantly warm water wash over his body. He remembered the cold of the water used for the drownings. Then he began to wash himself.

As he rinsed shampoo from his hair, his eyes on the drain, he realized what was wrong.

The water. Still soapy, with the water still running in the shower, he stepped out onto the bathmat, turned on the sink faucets, let the sink fill, then released the drain plug.

He stood there, shivering.

The water in the toilet, in the shower, in the bathroom sink went down the drain counterclockwise. Wherever he was, he was below the equator, somewhere in the southern hemisphere.

David Holden stepped back into the shower.

Cerillia assumed his own telephones were tapped. It was easy enough to do these days. For that reason, once the information had come, he had made no attempt to contact anyone with it, made no attempt to pass it on.

There was bank of public telephones in the lobby of the Hoover building, and he went to one of these. His driver was already waiting, to take him to the Oval Office at the White House to be roasted over the pit of Roman Makowski's self-inflated ego again. Cerillia still had his old office, still had a few administrative aides, but he was denied all access to FBI records, computers, field personnel. He told the aide with him, "Wait for me at the car."

The man nodded and walked off, but Cerillia noticed him looking over his shoulder. He was one of Makowski's men, of course. Cerillia picked up the phone, dialing directly, feeding quarters into the telephone from the broken roll in his left outside pocket.

"Mrs. Parrish. Is your husband there?"

"Who is this?"

"Just get him to the phone very quickly." If they knew about Lem Parrish he was pushing both Parrish and himself into the fire.

A man's voice. "Who is this?"

"Never mind that. Tell your friends this is the address and telephone number. Can you copy this down?"

"Just a moment. Who is this?"

"I'm giving it to you. You copy it or forget it." He read off the address from the torn-off daily calendar page. It was given to him as a Christmas gift. Each day there was a joke. Some of them were funny enough. Others were lame. He finished with the address and telephone number.

Lem Parrish asked again, "Who is this?"

Rudolph Cerillia hung up. He looked at the piece of paper in his hand. " 'Why did the chicken take an overdose of barbituiates?' " Cerillia read under his breath. " 'He had a suicide pact with the chicken who crossed the road.' "

Cerillia smiled, took a disposable lighter from his pocket as he exited into the cool air of the early fall, then lighted the piece of paper. He held it till the very last instant, then let it fall from his fingers. The aide and the driver were both watching him from beside the black Cadillac.

Rudolph Cerillia didn't care anymore.

"Very good of you to come, Mr. Cerillia."

Cerillia said nothing.

Roman Makowski cleared his throat. "I want you to feel at ease. You acted imprudently, but things can still be salvaged if you will cooperate. I have a tape recorder here that I will turn on, if you chose to cooperate, on which I will record everything you can tell me about these rightwing lunatics who call themselves the Patriots. Are you ready to begin?"

"No, Mr. Makowski, I'm not. No, sir."

Makowski looked at him oddly. "You refuse even to use my proper title?"

"There're a lot of proper titles for you, sir, but out of respect for the desk you sit behind, I won't say them. The President is still alive. Granted, you have the authority to sit in that chair. But to me it's immoral for you to attempt to unravel the entire administration as quickly as possible on the off chance that the President should survive."

"He won't survive, Cerillia. We both know that. Even if he does, he'd be a vegetable. The injuries he sustained when that Harrier crashed were so severe the doctors can't understand why he's still alive. And I've had about enough of your impudence."

Rudolph Cerillia stood up. "And I think I've had about enough of you. You can push me to resign until you're turning purple, but as long as that man whose chair you've expropriated is still alive, you're shit out of luck. You want to turn this country into something it doesn't want to be. And you can ram all the laws through Congress you can think of and make every executive order there's enough ink to print, but you won't change the will of the American people one iota."

Cerillia turned and started for the Oval Office door. Behind him, Makowski was saying "You just kissed your future good-bye, asshole."

Cerillia stopped at the doorway, but only for just a second. Makowski was shouting after him, "You can't leave without my dismissing you!" Cerillia looked over his shoulder as he opened the door, laughed, and walked out.

David Holden took the stairs slowly, the muscles in his stomach discouraging every step. The shoes—loafers— were comfortable enough and a good fit. They were expensive too. The clothes were the same, comfortable, well fitting, and not cheap.

Neither was the place where he was, wherever that happened to be. Along the upstairs corridor was a very narrow Oriental runner, looking to be the genuine article.

An identically patterned runner covered the center portion of the stair treads. The vase that held the flowers on top of the small table in the hallway looked expensive. The chandelier that dominated the hall at the base of the stairs was quite possibly genuine crystal. His wife would have known. She was good at that sort of thing. And thinking of Elizabeth suddenly made him think of Rosie. The two women were almost totally unalike. But there was something about them, something he could not put into words, that was the same. Perhaps it was only the way he loved them.

He stopped at the base of the stairs to catch his breath.

"Dr. Holden! You surprise me. I had not expected to see you up and about until the afternoon."

Holden turned too quickly toward the voice. The English was perfect, the accent—Spanish—perfect as well, like something out of an old Cesar Romero or Gilbert Roland movie. The man belonging to the voice looked like neither of those, however; he was about five and a half feet tall and nearly as thin as the cigar clenched in his gleeming white teeth.

He was standing in the doorway of what appeared to be a library and moved quickly toward Holden, smiling all the while. "So. May I walk beside you, Dr. Holden? You appear a bit unsteady."

"My stomach," Holden said truthfully.

"Yes—I had expected as much. It is a tribute to your iron will and sturdy constitution that you can move about at all so soon after your ordeal." He took the cigar from his teeth. "I will not offer you my hand, *señor,* because you would likely not take it and it would get our relationship off to a poor start. But, nevertheless, allow me to introduce myself. I am Juan Emiliano Ortega de Vasquez. I answer to all or any of my names." He smiled.

"What the hell's going on?" Holden said, looking at him.

"Let us retire to the library. I would offer you a drink, but it is early still and I fear that on an empty stomach the liquor might prove unpleasant. Coffee is the thing. And I like to drink it the American way so you need have no fear that it will be too strong." He walked beside Holden as he led David toward the library. "I wish your stay here to be pleasant and, for that to be, we must talk of many things."

"You're wasting your time—"

"Por favor!" Ortega de Vasquez raised his right hand palm outward as he smiled again. "Do me the courtesy of hearing me out, *señor.*"

Holden was too tired to argue.

He paused at the library doors, catching his wind again, his eyes moving about the room. Twelve-foot ceilings at least, floor-to-ceiling books, all of them with exquisite leather bindings. A wooden desk with leather trim dominated the center of the room, behind it floor-to-ceiling windows with heavy drapes of deep maroon, the drapes pulled back, allowing sunlight to filter through the light rose-colored sheers.

There was an inviting-looking leather wingback chair opposite the desk. Holden moved toward it, Ortega at his elbow.

Holden sank into the chair too quickly. A spasm of pain hit his stomach muscles.

"There is a medication I can provide to relieve the pain, *señor.*"

Holden looked up at him, licked his lips. "No—thank you."

Ortega smiled and seated himself in the leather swivel

chair behind the desk. "I will, as you Americans say, get right to the head."

"The point," Holden corrected.

"*Sí*—the point. No doubt you are disoriented."

"I'm somewhere south of the equator, presumably South America, and, considering that you speak Spanish instead of Portuguese, likely not Brazil. Considering the company you obviously keep, the possibilities narrow a bit more."

"*Bueno!*" Ortega smiled, actually clapping his hands together. "That is all you need to know for now too. How did you guess, though, that you were south of the equator, *señor?*"

"I flushed the toilet."

"Ha!" Ortega, looking genuinely amused, clapped his palm on the desk, the cigar dancing in his teeth. "You are resourceful, *señor.* Then indeed let me get, as you say, to the point. You are valuable. Removed from participation in the Patriots in your native land, you are valuable to us. You can, however, once again be valuable to yourself. Tell me this, *señor.* Which did you prefer? To awaken in a clean bed, well cared for, being free to move about as you wish? Or did you like the treatment offered you by Comrade Borsoi?"

Holden removed a cigarettes from his pack. Ortega moved to offer a lighter, but Holden nodded him off. "That's a silly question and a silly premise. I'm not free here. Can I leave this place? Can I walk on the grounds?"

"Assuredly, *señor,* as soon as you are well enough."

"How about beyond the hedge?"

Ortega smiled, gesturing expansively. "For the time being, señor, this must be your world. But you can find it a pleasant one."

"Right. What do you want?"

"I wish that you recover from your injuries. Then I wish that you speak to me truthfully concerning all that you know of your Patriots, naming names and places. And about the Federal Bureau of Investigation and its director, Rudolph Cerillia. About all those things that only you know which will be valuable to my comrades and myself. And then you will have a choice. Remain a prisoner, but a well-treated one, until the Front for the Liberation of America del Norte is in power. Then you will be free to go. Or you can make the wise decision and assist us in the making of certain videotapes aimed at the people of the United States. This accomplished, you will be free to go. You have many options. And, unfortunately, should you prove uncooperative, señor, I have options as well." For the first time a hint of menace crept into Ortega's voice.

"Let me ask you a question or two," Holden said, extinguishing the cigarette.

"As you will, *señor*." Ortega smiled.

"Fine," David Holden began. "If this is a bunch of happy comrades running the FLNA, how come I'm not in Cuba? Hmm? And if Borsoi is in charge of things in the United States, who's in charge of Borsoi?"

Ortega did not answer.

After the coffee, which was very good, Holden retired to his room, refusing Ortega's offer of help. As he entered his room, he saw her.

Very pretty, classically Latin, her hair in dark waves to her bare shoulders, wearing a loose, low-cut white blouse and a sweeping floral print skirt, she sat on the foot of his bed, which had been made in his absence.

"Can I help you?" he asked.

"I can help you, *señor*."

"How?" Holden leaned against the door jamb, half in, half out of the room.

"I was told about the terrible things that were done to you. And that you might be worried, worried about—" She let the sentence hang as she smiled, her eyes casting downward.

"You mean does my—"

"*Sí,*" she cut him off.

"Sweet of you to volunteer, Señorita—"

"Maria." She smiled.

"Somehow I knew it would be 'Maria,' Maria. Is it also possible that Señor Ortega wants to show me how happy I'll be if I cooperate?" Holden asked.

"I would try to make you happy, señor." Maria—or whatever her real name was—smiled.

"Gosh." Holden grinned. His stomach was hurting him very badly. He walked across the room and sat on the bed beside her. "What's a nice girl like you doing in a place like this?" he asked, keeping to the spirit of the conversation.

She smiled, saying nothing; but her left hand drifted from her lap to his right thigh and she looked up at him. The latter was hard to do. She was a tall girl and they sat on a sagging mattress and he was bent forward to ease the pain in his abdomen.

He told her, "Not that I'm not touched by your offer, Maria, but I'm not really as worried about my plumbing as I am my stomach at the moment."

"The doctor, he says that you are well."

"Yes. Señor Ortega told me the same thing."

"You do not think that I am clean? I have had the blood test, señor. It is safe to be with me."

"I doubt that," Holden told her honestly, holding her hand for a moment.

CHAPTER
27

Thomas Ashbrooke felt his wife nudging him. "Wake up, Tom. There's an overseas call."

He sat up in bed, a little too abruptly, disoriented for an instant. He'd been dreaming, seeing David and Elizabeth on their wedding day when suddenly men wearing masks and carrying submachine guns had broken into the church and begun killing people. Thomas Ashbrooke had been sitting in a front pew, a gun under his coat. But for some reason he was powerless to move and pull the gun and save the people who were getting killed on all sides of him, although no bullet touched him.

"It's an overseas call, Tom. She says she knows David."

Ashbrooke nodded, found his cigarettes beside the bed, lit one. Diane handed him the telephone receiver. "This is Tom Ashbrooke."

The voice on the other end of the line seemed to hesitate. Then: "Look. You don't know me. But I'm a close friend of David's and he's in trouble. You're his father-in-law, right?"

"Yeah. What kind of trouble? Who are you?"

"I don't even know if it's okay to talk."

"If David's in trouble I'll help." He looked at Diane. She had turned on the bedside lamp. "Go to the Rolodex. Get me one of the numbers outside the area."

"I understand." She nodded, already slipping out from beneath the covers, pulling a robe on over her nightgown. He was suddenly struck by how pretty she was. Elizabeth had always looked like her. "I'll pick up downstairs!" Diane sang back.

He spoke into the reciver again. "Look, young lady. My wife's going to give you a number. Call it in exactly thirty minutes." He looked at the Rolex on his wrist and compared it to the electronic digital on the nightstand. They were a minute apart. "Can you do that?"

"Yes."

"Are you using a pay phone?"

"Yes," she answered.

"Good. Find a different one. Get the number and call me in exactly thirty minutes from the moment you hang up." Ashbrooke's wife came on the line, and he hung up.

He moved barefoot across the floor, toward the closet, pulling out a shirt and a pair of trousers. He threw them on the bed. Then he crossed to the dresser and began pulling out underwear and socks. He stripped off his pajama bottoms and started to dress.

Diane came back into the bedroom. "I'll go with you."

"Fine. Get me a sweater. And dress warm."

He finished dressing, went back to the closet, pulled on a pair of low boots, and found a belt as well. When he looked back to the bed, there was a woolen sweater resting across it. "I'll just be a minute!" Diane called from the bathroom. He heard the toilet flush. She came out, already partially dressed in bra and panties and woolen knee socks. She looked good enough to eat, Ashbrooke reflected. "These cold mornings get you." She smiled, skinning into pink ski pants then a ridiculously heavy-looking white turtleneck sweater. Already Ashbrooke was loading one of the spare magazines for the Sig-Sauer P-226 9mm. "Is that really necessary?"

"I hope not," Ashbrooke answered his wife honestly.

"I'm ready."

They started out of the room.

The Porsche had gone from freezing to too hot in what seemed like minutes. Ashbrooke unzipped his coat. "Who do you think she was?" Diane asked, lighting a cigarette and passing it to him. She was trying to make certain he stayed awake, he realized.

"Odds are, David hasn't remained celibate since Elizabeth's death. Probably some woman in the Patriot underground that he works with." Ashbrooke downshifted into second as he took the corner and turned up the street toward the skating arena.

"It's hard to think of somebody—taking Elizabeth's place. I mean, I know it's the best for him, but . . ."

"To answer your question, I doubt that I would. But I'm a hell of a lot older than David."

She laughed, holding his hand over the shift knob for a moment, then releasing it as he started to upshift. The street was clear despite the premature dusting of snow earlier in the evening. He began dropping gears, coasting to a stop near the telephones. He looked at his watch. "Twenty-nine minutes. Not bad, sweetheart." He stepped out of the car, starting to tell her to wait for him, but she leaned across, killed the ignition, and started out.

He caught the door for her, helping her, then walked, Diane beside him, toward the telephones.

"Here are your keys."

As he took them, the third phone from the right began to ring. Ashbrooke walked over to it, looked up and down the street, and then picked it up. "Hello."

"This is Rose Shepherd. From before?"

"You're a friend of David's?"

"We're, ahh—"

"I understand. What's wrong?"

He realized he shouldn't have asked it that bluntly after he asked, because the woman's voice suddenly sounded odd, strained, as if she were holding back tears. "He might be dead and I don't know what to do and nobody else can help me, Mr. Ashbrooke, and—"

"Calm down. He's not dead. I'll help you." Diane held his hand.

CHAPTER
28

David Holden slept, forcing himself to awaken from the dream that replayed the nightmare he had really endured. He was bathed in sweat, nearly as cold as he had been in the dream.

There was little sun remaining and by the time he exited the shower, it was night. Close to the equator, he reasoned, for twilight is shorter the closer to the equator you go. That meant Peru or Bolivia or possibly even southern Ecuador, if his geography served him well. The closet was not exactly full of clothes, but apparently they anticipated that he'd be staying a long time. Several pairs of slacks, three pairs of shoes on the floor, a dozen shirts.

He picked the sturdiest of the pants, a khaki cotton twill. All of the trousers were made to be worn beltless, and no belt or necktie was available. He picked a dark-blue long-sleeved shirt, the only one with two breast pockets that buttoned closed. A pair of heavy cotton socks and the leather track shoes finished it off. Two handkerchiefs, one into each front pocket. On impulse, he took a second pair of socks from the drawer. He folded them separately, placing one in each hip pocket.

In a pinch they were thick enough to serve as a pad with a dressing.

The Rolex on his wrist indicated it was nearly eight, nearly time for the dinner Maria had mentioned before, when she had finally left, looking disappointed. She had suggested that perhaps they could make love after dinner. He'd told her they could decide later. Instead of climbing under the sheets, he'd pumped her as subtly as he could for information, realizing she would have been told not to tell him too much. But he had asked questions that he hoped were general enough not to arouse too much suspicion. Not things like "How many guards on the other side of the hedge?" but things like "Does all the staff—I mean, this house is huge—do they live here or in town?" From her answers he had gleaned a few possible facts. The house, or hacienda, was within traveling distance of a small city or large town. In answering him, Maria had volunteered that if none of the alcoholic beverages available suited him, they could get what he liked. The same for cigarette brands. He told her he had a terrible craving for some Salems and that his favorite whiskey was Jack Daniel's Black Label.

Though he had never liked menthol cigarettes or sour mash whiskey (he knew legions of people who did, of course), he had tried to pick two popular yet difficult-to-obtain brands in order to determine the size of the town nearby.

When Holden went down to dinner, Maria met him, in a red skirt and black lace-trimmed blouse, her black hair 90 percent up, the other 10 percent in little curls tantalizingly and randomly touching at her neck.

Ortega was already in the well-lighted, attractively appointed dining room. With Ortega was a man as gigantic as Oretega was diminutive. The two were engaged in conversation by closed French doors overlooking a plant-studded veranda.

"Dr. Holden! You look well rested."

Holden forced a smile. "I'm feeling a little better. I'm afraid I won't be the most enthusiastic eater, though; so my appologies in advance to your chef."

Ortega smiled graciously, stepping to the head of the table. Maria ushered Holden to one of two chairs on one side. He held hers for her, making not much more of a show of taking his time to sit down than he really felt. His stomach muscles still pained him terribly from the beatings with the boards.

The large man sat down opposite them. He looked like an oversized cherub, bulging cheeks, locks of curly hair framing his forehead above sparkling eyes. And he looked as if he was carrying a gun.

"You have not been introduced although you have met, *señors.* Dr. David Holden, may I present Señor Innocentio Hernandez."

"A pleasure, *señor.*" Hernandez smiled.

"The pleasure is all mine," Holden said affably. "Señor Ortega says we have met?"

Hernandez looked down into the fruit compote in the silver dish set at the middle of the silver-bordered dinner plate. "I am afraid, *señor,* you were not up to speaking at the time."

"Hmm." Holden nodded. He had no idea what his stomach would take in the way of solid food. Probably he'd been fed soft food somehow in the four days of his being out of it. But he would need carbohydrates. "I take it you delivered me here? Or helped?"

"*Sí.* That is it, *señor.* In a way, I suppose, although I do not ask for thanks, perhaps you might feel so inclined.

Had I left you with Dimitri Borsoi . . ." He let the proposition hang on the air as he smiled.

Holden waited for his host, then sampled the fruit, balls of melon, bits of citrus, light fare meant to sharpen the appetite. Two women and a formally attired butler served. Holden noticed no bulge under the butler's coat. So far Hernandez seemed to be the only one who was armed. Holden wondered why as he started making small talk while the courses were changed. "Señor Hernandez —you didn't happen to see what happened to my other things, did you?"

"Señor?"

"I mean, I was very happy to find my watch intact, but I was wondering about my weapons."

"You will not need them here, *señor.*" Hernandez smiled.

Holden was sick of smiling. "I was most particularly interested in my knife. I seem to remember firing out my pistols before I passed out from the gas. But did my knife survive?"

Hernandez looked at Ortega and so did Holden. Ortega nodded.

"Yes," Hernandez said after a long silence.

"Does Mr. Borsoi have it?"

"I fail to see the line of your questioning, *señor,*" Ortega interjected.

Holden ate the noodles—they were delicious—and picked at the beef, reasoning that he probably would be able to eat very little and the noodles would be more digestible and a better source of energy. "I have a certain sentimental attachment to it. I'm sure men like yourselves would understand that a prized weapon—one that is even named—is something of great value."

Innocentio Hernandez looked slightly embarrassed. Holden pressed. "Do you have it, sir?"

"*Sí.*"

"With you?"

This time Hernandez looked down at his food. Ortega spoke. "I am afraid, *señor,* that I cannot permit a weapon to you at this time."

"You named conditions this morning, *señor,*" Holden said, looking across the table at Ortega. "Should I decide to cooperate, there is one more condition. The knife is returned to me." He made up a story, but one that he hoped sounded convincing. "The knife was a present to me from my wife and three children on my birthday just before their deaths." It was not. "My son washed cars to help earn some of the money," Holden embroidered. "My older daughter did baby-sitting for her share. It means a great deal to me. You have asked that I consider your proposals. I ask that you consider my honor in this slight way if I am to compromise my honor in other ways."

Hernandez looked more embarrassed than before.

Ortega looked at Hernandez, who shrugged. Ortega nodded. Then Hernandez stood, reaching under his coat with his left hand. Holden saw the flash of the shoulder holster. It was his own. The Defender knife appeared in Hernandez's massive hand. He set it on the table beside the centerpiece. "*El cuchillo, señor.*"

Holden did not reach for it. Ortega spoke. "I shall take personal charge of this fine blade, *señor,* returning it to you after you have fulfilled your side of what I take may well be an agreement. Until then consider me merely the custodian of your property."

"May I, ahh—"

Ortega coughed, said, "Certainly. But should you attempt, *señor,* to—"

"Please." Holden nodded. Slowly he reached for the knife, watching Hernandez, who moved much closer, obviously armed and too big to be ignored. Holden closed his fingers over the haft of the knife, raising it before him, watching the blade as it caught the light.

"It is fine steel, *señor,*" Hernandez said. "A man like Dimitri Borsoi does not understand such matters. It speaks well of you, *señor,* that you do understand such things." He sounded genuinely moved.

Holden returned the Crain knife to the center of the table and picked up his fork. "Thank you, *señors.* I tire. But I'm still hungry."

"Whatever you wish, *señor.*" Ortega nodded.

Holden ate all of the noodles and a piece of bread, drank half a glass of the red wine that was served with dinner. With Maria helping him to walk, he retired to the library with the men. Awaiting him there was a fresh pack of Salems and a bottle of Jack Daniel's Black Label.

If he were ever going to escape, it would have to be tonight. And he would have to get the knife, because the pistol Innocentio Hernandez carried seemed to be the only gun in the house, and Holden's knife, once Hernandez was gone, would be the only weapon. Dinner conversation had revealed that Hernandez lived in the guest house near the estate's main entrance. Holden considered that a good place to avoid, for despite his relaxed, pleasant manner, there was something under the surface in Hernandez, something very deadly.

CHAPTER
29

He lay across his bed, fully dressed, satisfied that no cameras watched him. Fiber optics were possible, of course, but he would have to take his chances.

At one in the morning he got up, went to the bathroom, brushed his teeth, and lit a cigarette—not one of the menthol ones, however. He began clipping off six-foot lengths of dental floss from the almost new, two hundred–yard package. Each six-foot strand he would wrap around the bedpost at the three-foot mark. Each ten six-foot lengths he would wind together to form a single wider strand. He set these aside until he had three such pieces. By now it was nearly one thirty. He spent the next half hour braiding them together into a single cord approximately two and a half feet long. It would have been simpler to use a length of bedding or even a towel, but he was not at full strength.

The garrote made from the dental floss would bite into the neck because it was narrow, whereas a sheet would have required crushing the larynx with a well-placed Thugee knot or by sheer brute force.

There were always electrical appliance cords, for the

lamp or clock, for example. But as he had been allowed
no belt, it was likely that if he unplugged one of the
lamps an alarm would sound. He couldn't risk that.

When he was through, Holden had a handy garrote
and his mind was fully alert. He went to the bedding
next, tearing the sheet into lengthwise strips, which he
knotted together to form a rope.

Maria had tried again and if it hadn't been for Rosie,
Holden would have made love with her. He did wonder if
he was all right, and she was very pretty. And, considering the circumstances, it might be the last time he'd be
with a woman before his death. But on the slight chance
he would make it alive, he realized he would have felt
terribly guilty if he had betrayed Rosie. They had talked
for a while, Holden pumping her a little more. Maria was
willing to talk more than before because of the things
Holden had said about his family. She had actually cried
when she said how sorry she was that his wife and three
children had been killed.

For that, he would endeavor to avoid killing her. But
Maria had spoken about many things, among which how
she enjoyed going to the beach. Peru or Ecuador, then.
That much he knew.

At two-thirty in the morning, after watching the
grounds from his darkened window for half an hour,
David Holden went to his door. There was no sign of
guards on the grounds but there were occasional beams
of light from beyond the hedgerow, perhaps automobile
headlights. If he could steal a car, that would be a definite
plus in his debilitated condition.

No key had been turned in his lock. But, to guard
against a lock-in, he had taken the filters of two cigarettes
and stuffed them into the hole for the bolt. By reducing
the depth to which the bolt could penetrate in this way,

Holden enhanced the chances that he'd be able to break it clear. It was not necessary. With all the lights in his room out, Holden simply opened the door and peered into the hallway.

At the head of the stairs stood a man, smoking a cigarette. Holden watched him long enough to ascertain that he was dropping the ashes into his hand. If he was stationed there as a guard there would have been an ashtray. The man turned a bit and Holden drew back, but caught a glimpse of his face. It was the burly butler. There was no indication the man was armed.

To the left along the hallway was a window, but if it matched the drop from his room it would not be easy for David to navigate in his present condition. He could have punched out his window screen and used the sheet rope to let himself down onto the grounds, but if Ortega was so careless about security in the house itself, the grounds surrounding it were probably doubly dangerous. He could not, in his physical state, attempt to cross the grounds weaponless. There could be jungle beyond the hedge, animals as well as men to kill him.

Holden drew back into his room.

They were counting on his poor physical condition to make him behave. No guns in the house were insurance against his action despite his weakened state. Which meant that it had to be tonight, because in a few nights the situation would change dramatically, especially once they were certain he would not voluntarily cooperate. And he had no intention of selling out the Patriots or his country.

The garrote. The man at the head of the stairs. If the man didn't move on, it would have to be that. They would suspect an escape attempt least of all tonight because he had, with much talking, convinced Ortega he was interested in a tour of the grounds tomorrow morning if they could rest several times. And that would have spelled out to Ortega that Holden was planning to reconnoiter before any escape attempt. Tonight was definitely the night.

But the pain in his stomach was real. It would slow him, reduce his stamina.

With the rope of sheet strips crossbody from right shoulder to left hip, the dental floss garrote in his fists, Holden looked again through the doorway and into the hallway. He waited now for the butler to finish his cigarette and be on his way.

It took another three minutes. By now the cigarette presumably was burned to flesh-searing length, but at last the butler walked down the stairs. Apparently the man had been told to take a look around before retiring.

Holden hoped he was through looking.

Ortega had locked the Defender knife in his top desk drawer. If it was still there, then the library or the desk itself had to have some sort of alarm system. That meant Oretega himself would be required.

Holden edged through the doorway, along the corridor, keeping close to the wall. The chandelier at the center of the downstairs hall glowed dully, like some giant night-light. Holden reached the end of the corridor. It branched to his right, he assumed toward Ortega's rooms.

Holden peered around the corner, saw no one, then continued on.

On the left side of the hallway was the bannister overlooking the main hall; on the right were several doors. The only way to discover which room belonged to Ortega was to try each door. As Holden moved, he looked for photoelectric eyes as part of some sort of alarm system.

None were in evidence. He stepped back from the first door and crouched. No bar of light was visible beneath it. Holden stood to his full height too fast and doubled over onto his knees with cramps.

His breathing came hard, so loud he thought that at any second he would be heard.

Holden simply knelt there in the darkness for what might have been several minutes, powerless to stand. At last the cramps eased and, slowly this time, he stood. Breathing hard and bathed in cold sweat, he tried the first door. The knob turned easily under his hand.

His eyes well accustomed to the darkness, it was simple enough to determine that the room was unoccupied. He closed the door as quietly as he could, then moved on.

The next door showed light beneath it.

Holden tried it. The knob turned easily. He peered through a small crack between the door and the jamb, seeing no sign of anyone inside the room. He considered the bathroom. As he let himself in, he noticed several things. From the items on the mirrored dresser, it was obviously a woman's room. And obviously the bed had not been used that night.

He checked the bathroom. A douche bag was beside the tub. A curling iron was on the sink. He walked back into the bedroom. A quick glance into the closet confirmed that it was Maria's room. He recognized the outfit she had worn earlier in the evening.

Nowhere in the room was there evidence of a robe or slippers. Although in the warm climate she might not have used a robe, and she might have preferred to move about barefoot, he assumed that she had not left the house but merely left her room. The butler didn't seem quite up to her speed, nor had any of the other male servants he'd seen about the house. She had to be with Ortega. There were two more doors in the hallway.

Holden let himself out, standing beside the wall for a few moments until his eyes once again became accustomed to the darkness.

He walked on, the pain in his stomach lessening a little with cautious movement. The next door was dark, but rather than trying it he moved on, looking for light under the last door. He found it.

Slowly he tried the knob.

The door was locked. If it had been a movie, he smiled ruefully, a set of lock picks would have appeared magically from his pocket or, better still, the door wouldn't have been locked in the first place. If he tried a solid kick against the door, he might never be able to move, with stomach muscles as tender as his were.

Holden shrugged, moved back toward the railing, and launched himself toward the door with full body force. Stomach muscles be damned, it was now or never.

His right shoulder, upper body, and right hip impacted the center of the door and it sprang inward. Holden lost his balance, sprawling across the floor, the door slamming against the wall. It was some sort of elaborate sitting room. His stomach was killing him. He tried to stand.

Ortega appeared in a doorway leading off to the left. "You are a fool, *señor!*" As Ortega started to move, Holden picked himself up although he was doubled over with cramps, then threw himself toward the much smaller man. He impacted the same way he had the door, bowling Ortega back through the doorway.

The man crumpled under Holden's weight.

Holden rolled off him, doubled over uncontrollably with stomach cramps. Ortega was up, wiping the blood away from his mouth with the back of his hand. He started to kick toward Holden's face. Holden blocked as best he could, but it was a feeble effort, as the pain in his abdomen still consumed him.

He heard a crashing sound. Pottery or something smashing. Ortega sagged to his knees, then fell forward, his head inches from Holden's own. Standing behind him was Maria. She was stark naked, in her hands the remnants of a bowl identical to the one Holden had seen earlier in the hallway with the flower arrangement.

"Hi," Holden said, not knowing what else to say.

"Will you take me with you, *señor?*"

"Can you figure out how to keep the servants from checking up here with all the noise I made?"

"Sí." She threw the rest of the broken pottery bowl onto the carpet, then covered her pubic hair with her hands.

Holden tried to stand, couldn't. "Tell me where he keeps a gun in his room."

"There are no guns here, *señor.*" She was pulling a nightgown over her head, long, very feminine-looking, then she stepped into slippers. She started for the door. "In my room, *señor.* Quickly." She grabbed up a robe but didn't put it on.

She stood in the doorway and shrieked. "I will never let you do that again, Emiliano! Pig!" Some words in Spanish followed that Holden had never heard before but they didn't sound nice. The door slammed.

Holden was on his knees. Mechanically he checked Ortega for a pulse. He found one easily enough. With the rope of sheet strips, Holden, still unable to stand, quickly bound and gagged him.

He could hear Maria shouting from the corridor outside, the same sort of vituperations he'd heard before she'd slammed the door.

The servants would be smart enough to avoid Ortega if he were having women troubles—Holden hoped. Finally he was able to stand.

After a few seconds of weaving, he got his equilibrium and began to search the room. Maria was right. No gun was in evidence. But there were keys, one of which looked like an alarm key. Holden pocketed those. None were car keys. No incriminating documents. A box of prophylactics, a plastic bag of marijuana and some cigarette papers for rolling, and some cigars were the only noteworthy items.

Holden checked his watch. Ortega was starting to come around. Holden didn't much care. Bound and gagged, he'd keep for a while. But it was time to try to make it to Maria's room.

Holden left the bedroom, made a quick search of the sitting room, and remembered the bathroom. Ortega, after all, wasn't a prisoner, and his pencil-thin mustache wasn't maintained with an electric razor.

In the bathroom was a straight razor.

David Holden smiled.

Maria was dressed in blue jeans and a T-shirt, looking more like Rosie Shepherd than the fiery Latin temptress look she had tried for earlier. "I was beginning to think you would not come, *señor.*"

"David. I came. How do we get out of here? There's not much time left before dawn."

"It is impossible, *señor*—David."

"Then why are you dressed like that? Why'd you ask me to take you with me?"

"I must get away. They are evil men. I know what

happens to other women before me, David. They are given drugs, and after a time they are thrown out onto the streets of the town or killed. It is better to be killed."

Holden looked away from her, looked down at the straight razor in his left hand. He looked back into her eyes. "I need to get into his desk. I need my knife. This is fine for slitting somebody's throat close up, but we might need more than that. And there must be some things in his library that'd be useful. Is this the key to turn off the alarm in the library?" He held up the alarm key for her to see.

"I have seen him use it."

"Good. Where are we?"

"Sixty kilometers north of Iquitos."

"Peru?"

"*Sí*—Republica de Peru."

Holden nodded. He tried to remember his geography. Iquitos was near the headwaters of the Amazon, he thought. He shook his head. "Downstairs, check the library then we make a break for it."

"*Sí.*" Maria smiled.

Holden made a mental note to ask her if that was her real name.

They encountered no one along the stairs or in the main hall below. There was a small brass light switch cover that slipped to the side and, beneath it, lay the alarm switch. Holden used the key. He was confident he had shut the alarm off because the key would turn only one way and, if Ortega has locked his bedroom door, he would have secured the library as well—Holden hoped.

Inside the library, David went immediately to the desk. "Close the door, Maria."

He tried several likely-looking keys until he found the

correct one for the center drawer. Then he opened the drawer and reached in for his knife.

Keeping his voice low, Holden asked Maria, who had come to stand near him along the opposite side of the desk, "Have you ever seen a gun in this house, aside from Hernandez's?"

At the mention of his name she made the sign of the Cross. "Once I saw Emiliano with a gun. I do not know where it came from."

Holden's eyes scanned the room. At any moment a servant up early or for some other reason might pass by and notice lights from beneath the door. Or someone on the grounds would see lights through the windows. The books. "Does Ortega read a great deal?"

"He collects these things, *señor*. He does not read them. He is a stupid man."

"What kind of gun was it you saw?"

"I know nothing about guns, David."

"I mean, a handgun? Or bigger?"

"Bigger."

Holden walked toward the wall, telling Maria, "Start looking for a button or a switch anywhere along these bookcases." He started with the interior side wall first.

It took almost half an hour. Holden was about to give up when Maria called out in a loud stage whisper, *"Señor!"* As quickly as he could without aggravating his stomach muscles, he crossed the room to stand beside her. "Here, *señor*."

Behind a beautifully bound volume of *Don Quixote* was a hollow. Inside the hollow was a button. Holden should have noticed the book earlier. Of all the books he had moved aside or seen there, it was the only one showing even the slightest wear to the binding.

Holden pushed the button. For all he knew, it could have been an alarm.

But instead the wall section—books, bookshelves, and all—slipped back, then left, disappearing behind the bookshelves immediately beside it. There was a light switch. Holden activated it.

The walls to the left, right, and rear were lined with racks of firearms.

David Holden smiled even more than he had when he'd found the straight razor.

He entered the room, carefully lest there be some trap, but there seemed to be none. All of the rifles were M-16s. A dozen of them. Shotguns, equally as many, all of them Remington 870s. A section of wall was pegboard; on wooden pegs were an assortment of handguns, all of them large-capacity 9mms. Apparently Ortega was somewhat of a collector. Holden found a Beretta 92F, all but brand new, and took it down from the pegs. A small cabinet beneath the handguns held boxes of ammunition. On shelves immediately below the rifles and handguns were spare magazines. Holden shoved the empty Beretta into his trouser band, remembering too late his tender abdomen. The pain caused him to lean across the shelf.

"Señor David? What is it?"

"My stomach. I'll be all right. Take down three of those rifles. Over there, the ones withh the handles on top. Then from the shelf beneath them I want eighteen of the magazines. Find a sack or something. If you have to, use my knife—it's on the desk—and cut off the leather from one of the chairs or the bottom of the drapes. We need something to carry this stuff."

"All of it?"

He smiled as he took the first M-16 from here and

began to load the magazine already up the well with 5.56mm ball.

An M-16 slung from each side, an expensive leather briefcase in his left hand, and both the borrowed Beretta and his knife in his trouser band—the knife beside his hip to minimize danger to himself—Holden walked from the library into the hallway. It had taken time to disassemble and neutralize all the weapons, but he felt better without having them at his back. Maria—what *was* her real name?—carried an 870 and the third M-16, a second Beretta in her waistband.

It was dawn as Holden opened the front door and stepped into the outside world. Beyond the hedges lay freedom and possibly death. He was willing to risk the latter for the sake of the former. "Let's leave this place," Holden almost whispered.

CHAPTER
30

Gravel crunched under their feet as they walked. "How was I brought here?"

"The airplane, Señor David."

Holden stopped walking. "What kind of airplane and where is it?"

"I do not know."

"What kind, or where it is?"

"I know where it is. Just down the road that way." Maria gestured toward the north beyond the hedge.

"Have you seen it?"

"*Sí.*"

"Does it have propellers?"

"Oh, *sí.*"

"Is it very big?"

"It is about—" She seemed to be looking around for something to compare it to. Unless it was the same size as the main house or a tree, she was out of luck, Holden mused.

"One propeller or two?"

"Two."

He had never soloed a twin-engine aircraft, and they

were more complicated than single engines. "How far down the road, Maria?"

"Less than a kilometer."

"Are you sure it is still there?"

"Oh, *sí.*"

Holden kept walking toward the hedge. At last they were off the gravel driveway. The sun was peeking up. Maria was humming a little tune under her breath, barely audible. He guessed she was terrified, which made excellent sense under the circumstances.

They reached the hedge.

"Stay behind me and be quiet," he told her, then stopped for a moment. "Say, is your name really Maria?"

She seemed to blush, but he told himself it was hard to tell for sure in the gray light. "Yes, David."

Holden smiled, trying to sound more positive than he felt as he said, "We'll get out of this; we'll reach that plane and make it out." She leaned up and kissed him on the cheek. "What was that for?"

"For being the first man who did not just want—" She looked away.

He supposed that was a compliment. David Holden started walking again, not pushing his speed, conserving his strength, for the pain was making him a little light-headed. But walking did seem to help ease the pain.

There was a break in the hedge near the driveway and Holden whispered into her ear, "What's beyond the hedge?"

"The bunkhouse. The small house he—"

"Who?"

She crossed herself. "Innocentio Hernandez."

"Why are you so afraid of him? Just because he's so big?"

"He is a communist. He is a drug smuggler. He is a

killer. I saw him wring a man's neck once like a man might kill a chicken. He is very bad, Señor David. With guns and knives and fists and feet. He is very bad."

Holden assumed that meant Hernandez was very good, a very formidable opponent. "What else is beyond the hedge?" He should have asked her that first thing, he realized, but he wasn't functioning at anywhere near 100-percent efficiency. All he really wanted to do was lie down beside Rosie Shepherd and sleep.

"The garage. There are cars and trucks."

"How many men in the bunkhouse?"

"Maybe twenty, señor."

"Gunmen or workers?"

"They are both, señor."

"Wonderful."

Holden signaled her to stay behind, then edged forward along the hedge toward the break for the driveway.

He peered beyond the hedge. The driveway extended for another eighth of a mile until it passed through a high chainlink fence. There were men standing beside the gate, armed with M-16s. More were visible by the instant as the sun rose.

Halfway between the hedge and the fence on the left was a small house, where he assumed Hernandez lived. On the right was a larger, less well made structure, with a lower roof. There were large window air conditioners visible at the front and the back, three on each side. The bunkhouse.

Beside the gate was a low doorless structure, like a stable, but instead of horses it housed cars.

He could hot-wire a car, punch it through the fence, and get to the airfield. But the guards at the gate had to be taken care of. And it would be a shooting job. So much for his garrote, but making it had passed the time.

He ducked back, edged toward Maria, whispered, "I'm going out there, getting as close as I can to the guards by the gate. As soon as you hear me shout, run for the garage. Don't stop for anybody. If you beat me to it, look for a sturdy vehicle—"

"I do not know this word, Señor David."

"Big—strong. Like Innocentio Hernandez." He smiled. "If there are keys in it or on a board on the wall, wonderful. If not, see if you can find a wrench or hammer or something."

"Sí, señor."

He kissed her forehead. "Don't worry," Holden lied. Both M-16s were chamber-loaded. He set down the briefcase, telling Maria, "Don't forget it, huh?" He worked both safety tumblers to auto before closing his fists on the pistol grips.

"Go with God, Señor David."

"Thank you," Holden whispered.

Pulling himself erect, using the pain to sharpen his senses, Holden walked toward where the driveway and hedge met. He took a deep breath. He thought of Rosie and of Elizabeth and their children. And he thought of Rufus Burroughs too.

Holden stepped around the corner of the hedge, walking down the driveway.

He couldn't run for much distance, anyway. And the steadier he was, the steadier he could shoot. The two guards at the gate were talking. He could hear them just faintly. He kept walking, the gravel crunching under his feet louder than their voices.

There was no sound of anyone stirring in the bunkhouse, or of any activity from the house where Innocentio Hernandez, the man who strangled men like chickens, lived.

Holden kept walking.

He smiled to himself. Somebody needed to be whistling and Lee Van Cleef needed to be at the other end of the driveway. And instead of M-16s, Holden needed a Winchester lever action and a Colt Single Action Army.

The sun would be behind him, more or less. That was always good in the westerns. He kept walking, the distance between himself and the two men at the gate now less than seventy-five yards.

In a second one of them would turn and it would start. He knew that. He kept walking.

One of them turned, shouted something in Spanish that Holden didn't understand. Holden shoved both M-16s out tight against their slings and opened fire.

Gunfire tore into the ground behind him and to the right as a guard started shooting. Holden kept firing. The first guard who had sounded the alarm was down, then the second man.

"Run for it, Maria!"

Then Holden himself started to run, sounds and light coming from the bunkhouse, lights coming on in the bunkhouse, a solitary light flashing on from Innocentio Hernandez's house.

Holden's breath came in short gasps.

He neared the garage, looked back, saw Maria running toward the garage and men coming from the bunkhouse. One was already on the bunkhouse steps raising a rifle to his shoulder. Holden let the second M-16 fall to his side, shouldered the one in his right hand, and fired a three-round burst toward the rifleman, spilling him over the side of the steps and out of sight. Maria kept running.

Holden surveyed the vehicles. The largest was a white Chevy Suburban. If memory served, some of them had monstrous V-8s. His abdomen was paining him terribly, but he jogged toward the vehicle.

Holden stepped up on the running board. He was in luck, keys were in the ignition. He opened the door, did a standing mechanic's start. The engine stuttered for a moment, then roared to life reassuringly as he pumped the gas pedal again.

Maria was nearing the garage.

Suddenly on the porch of the small house Holden saw Hernandez, a G-3 assault rifle with a scope mounted on it coming up in his hands. Hernandez shouted, *"Puta!"*

Holden shouldered the M-16 and smiled.

As Hernandez attempted to fire, Holden fired first. Hernandez's rifle fell from his hands as he grabbed at his left thigh, stumbled, and fell. Holden sprayed out both rifles into the tires of the other vehicles, giving each at least one flat, then threw both rifles into the front seat and climbed behind the wheel. He doubled over the steering wheel with pain. Then, recovering slightly, he released the parking brake as he threw the automatic transmission into drive and let the vehicle move forward, the automatic choke still running as the vehicle gathered momentum.

Maria ran toward him. Holden glanced at the passenger door. It was unlocked. She ran for it and pulled it open. Holden stomped the gas and cut the wheel hard right as she fell in beside him. The M-16s lay between them with the briefcase with the spare magazines on the floor at her feet. "Down on the floor. Change magazines in both rifles like I told you. Stay down!"

Holden cut the wheel left, away from the gates. Men were pouring out of the bunkhouse now. Hernandez limped down the steps of his house, a pistol in his right fist, firing toward them. A bullet glanced off the hood of the Suburban, spiderwebbing the windshield at the bottom.

Holden began a long arc left, keeping his speed constant, turning past the bunkhouse. Holden ducked, shouting to Maria, "Stay down!" Gunfire streamed toward them, glass shattering in the windows of the Suburban, bullets *ping*ing off the body work, punching through the doors, into the seat, into the dashboard as he accelerated.

The gate. Men ran toward the Suburban, but Holden used the vehhicle's tonnage to swat them away.

He locked the steering wheel in his left fist and dropped to a lower gear, revving the engine. The entire vehicle seemed to hesitate. Holden popped the selector back into drive mere feet from the gate, then tucked down, his abdominal muscles screaming in protest, as sheets of chainlink crashed over the hood, across the roof. Gunfire from behind shattered the rear glass.

They were through.

CHAPTER
31

The Suburban, its radiator still spewing steam from where it had been punctured, was a hundred yards away.

Holden ran the list in his head again, certain he'd forgotten something. There was no manual aboard to double check himself. He'd disabled the emergency locator transmitter in the event they were forced down and Ortega and Hernandez had enough clout to get official help in a search. He'd set the parking brake, turned all switches to off, set trim tabs to zero.

Only one of the doors was secured. He left the second open for Maria, who would pull the chocks.

Tie-downs had been severed. He'd ignored lights and beacons. The cabin air inlet was working. Antennas checked, air outlet functional. The fuel sumps were drained. Ailerons, flaps, and trim tabs all checked out.

Fuel checked, the plane's tanks topped off, confirming his suspicion that it was being readied for use. Oil was topped off as well.

Both engine air intakes checked.

He wasn't remembering something, he told himself. But he had to be.

Landing gear, oxygen.

It had to be everything.

He checked the parking brake. Set. Oxygen. He checked it again. Landing gear handle. Down.

He set the cowl flap switches on and set the selector valves to main. Then he did a visual on circuit breakers and switches.

He flipped the battery switch on.

He checked main and auxiliary tanks again; both topped off. He set the fuel quantity selector to main.

Landing gear position lights checked.

He opened the throttle about halfway, setting the prop controls to low pitch, giving him the highest RPMs for takeoff. The auxiliary fuel pump he set on high while he built pressure.

His mixture was at full rich.

Holden turned the magneto to start, shouting out the vent window to Maria, "Move the chocks now! Watch for the propellers!" She nodded that she understood. Her hair was tossed in the backdraft as she removed first one, then crossed behind the plane to remove the second. She tossed them in aft and climbed aboard. "Secure the door, Maria!"

He watched his RPMs, playing the throttle to idle RPMs.

Oil pressure was at twenty-five PSI.

He flipped the alternator switch on, checking his panels again.

Already he was starting the second engine.

He released the brakes, checked that they worked.

Maria came forward, slipped into the copilot's seat. "Buckle up, Maria!"

Auxiliary fuel pumps off. He adjusted engine richness

by guessing at the elevation. Each prop was hovering near 2,200 RPMs.

"Señor David! Look!"

Holden twisted in his seat, looking out the starboard window beside her.

Two pickup trucks and a car were approaching with men hanging from the backs of the trucks, assault rifles and shotguns in their hands.

"Shit!"

"What?"

"Mierda, I think!"

"Ohh, *sí."*

Holden moved the throttles, checking the magnetos for maximum drop. He reduced from 1,700 RPMs to 1,500, feathering his props, watching for RPM drop. It was not excessive, he hoped.

Throttles to idle.

He checked his trim.

"They are coming, *señor!"*

Maria was a classic hysteric, her voice rising in pitch each time she uttered a new warning. He could see them, less than two hundred yards now.

He set the flaps for takeoff and released the parking break.

Full throttle now. David glanced at his oil temeperature. It was nearly high enough.

As the aircraft taxied forward, Holden corrected fuel flow for altitude, accelerating as much as he dared now. The trucks were splitting up, trying to cut him off. Holden was building to airspeed. No winds. He could see the aircraft's shadow, a streak of black on the bleached gray of the tarmac.

There was no fence, only high jungle canopy and jagged outcroppings of granite racing toward them.

Gunfire was coming from both sides, the trucks flanking them, the car ahead of them, slowing down, trying to force Holden to cut airspeed. Holden took the Beretta from the waistband of his trousers, stabbed it through the still-open storm vent with his left hand, and fired across the nose of the aircraft toward the rear of the car. It swerved, didn't veer off or speed up.

"Maria. Just hold on." Holden increased speed as gunfire came from the rear of the car now on both sides. The window near Maria's head spiderwebbed and she screamed. Holden glanced right at the riflesmen in the truck bed.

Bullets *ping*ed off the fuselage.

A burst ripped across the starboard engine cowling, but there were no instrument problems.

He was at full throttle now, the aircraft starting to climb. He stuffed the Beretta under his thigh, reached to the landing gear handle, and yanked, pulling up as he hauled back as hard as he could on the yoke.

They were airborne.

Gunfire blasted from the ground below. Holden banked steeply to starboard, trying to avoid the trees and at the same time avoid a direct pass over the field.

He was gaining altitude.

Maria screamed at the same instant Holden saw gasoline spraying from the portside engine. He was losing RPMs. Holden checked airspeed. It was dropping below 120 mph. He closed the portside throttle and started feathering the portside propeller.

"We are going to crash!"

"We'll be all right," Holden lied.

He powered up the starboard engine. Airspeed was barely 115 mph. They were clear of the field, flying over hilly terrain with dense tree cover and more granite outcroppings. He was losing altitude. Holden began securing the inoperative engine.

The electrical load on the starboard engine was increasing.

His eyes drifted across the control panel. Oil temperature in the starboard engine was going up fast.

Holden maintained altitude, his eyes scanning the ground.

He smelled oil burning. He checked the oil temperature. It was rising, pressure falling.

"We're going to set down," Holden announced, still not certain where.

They were skimming the treetops now. Suddenly the aircraft was over a deep valley, a ribbon of blue green at its approximate center, winding southeastward. As the altimeter spun, Holden brought the nose up slightly, coasting downward.

There was a stretch of reddish-brown ground below to his left, where most of the foliage seemed to have been cut away or burned. Holden angled the aircraft toward it.

He looked at Maria. She was saying her rosary.

Holden lowered the landing gear.

The reddish-brown spot was coming up fast.

He gave himself fifteen degrees of flap, checked his airspeed; just over a hundred.

He throttled back.

The ground was racing toward them. He could see the aircraft's shadow on the ground, the sun behind them.

It wasn't solid.

Holden started powering up. There was a buzzing sound and he looked to the starboard engine. Flames.

"Pray for me too!" Too late to pull out. Holden went full flaps down as he throttled back, the landing gear

touching, the aircraft lurching forward and right, spin-
ning, Holden's head slamming against the window.

Smoke. David Holden smelled it. As he opened his
eyes, he saw it and could almost feel it around him.

He looked up, the left side of his head hurting badly,
feeling sticky with blood.

Maria. "Maria?"

"I hurt, *señor.*"

She was still strapped in. Holden tried his seat restraint. It opened. He could move, half falling from the
seat as he did, the pain in his abdomen returning. He
licked his dry lips with his dry tongue and coughed, making the pain still worse.

The smoke. The starboard engine had caught fire.

He tried moving. His hands were on Maria's shoulders,
then to her waist. The seat restraint wouldn't budge.
Holden reached to the suitcase between his seat and
Maria's and knelt beside her. He saw floaters across his
eyes as the pain increased. Inside the bag was his knife.
He caught it up in his hand, then used it to cut her free of
the webbing.

"Where do you hurt, Maria?"

"Everywhere."

She was crying, sounded hysterical and might not have
been seriously hurt at all. "Wiggle your toes. Try that."

"They wiggle, *señor.*"

Holden looked up. The starboard engine, only half visible above the mud and mire into which the plane had
crashed, was burning.

Holden helped her from the seat and she screamed. If
her toes wiggled, he told himself, her back couldn't be
broken. "Come on!" Holden tossed the briefcase aft. The
rifles and the shotgun were already there.

He remembered to reach back for his pistol, stuffed it inside his right front pocket.

The smoke was worse now, crackling sounds coming from the control panels.

He'd shut down power; somehow he remembered doing that. So it had to be insulation or plastic, not wiring that was burning.

With Maria ahead of him, Holden worked his way aft. "Grab a rifle. Forget the shotgun." He slung it to her. She was crying.

Holden grabbed up two rifles, slinging them crossbody one on each side. He opened two buttons at the front of his shirt, sticking spare magazines from the case inside, stuffing his pockets with them as many as he could carry.

There was a puffing sound. He could see flames more clearly now from the engine.

Holden tried the doors. With force—he almost fell through—they opened.

Mud, like a swamp, reeking fetidly.

The sun beat down.

The men in the trucks at the airfield. They would have seen the crash or heard it and would be coming soon.

Holden said to Maria, "Hold my hand and don't let go. Got it?"

"*Sí!*"

His knife in his teeth, Holden started to climb down. Doubling up with the cramps, half falling from the fuselage, catching himself with his hands on the door.

He was in the mud, well past his waist, but beneath the mud it seemed a little solid. He looked around. The closest escape from the mud was toward the east.

"Come on," he said through clenched teeth.

Maria half fell into his arms. Holden, staggering back,

kept her upright. She was still weeping. Holding her by the hand, he dragged her away from the aircraft.

The crackling sounds were louder now and he smelled gasoline more than before.

He tried to quicken their pace.

The mud was shallower. He kept moving, his abdominal muscles knotting. He kept going, dragging her behind him.

The ground beneath the mud began to rise.

Holden staggered a few more paces, dragging Maria to him as he heard the roar beginning. He collapsed into the mud, keeping her head above it as the roar and then a rush of searing heat washed over them.

She wept in his arms.

David Holden looked back. A black-and-orange fireball gushed upward, engulfing the fuselage of the twin-engine aircraft.

Holden stabbed his knife into the drier ground at arm's length, then started to drag them toward it.

For the moment they were alive. For the moment they were free.

David Holden got to his knees then his feet, grabbing up the Defender knife.

Their bodies were covered with the reddish ooze, his weapons clogged with it.

The guns would clean.

There was a river nearby. He'd seen it from the air. "Come on, Maria. Just a little farther," Holden lied to her once again.

One foot after the other. She leaned heavily against him. They kept moving. "We're free, Maria. Keep going."